IJB

D0865943

000000925500

SPECIAL MESSAGE TO READERS

THE ULVERSCROFT FOUNDATION
(registered UK charity number 264873)
was established in 1972 to provide funds for
research, diagnosis and treatment of eye diseases.
Examples of major projects funded by
the Ulverscroft Foundation are:-

- The Children's Eye Unit at Moorfields Eye Hospital, London
- The Ulverscroft Children's Eye Unit at Great Ormond Street Hospital for Sick Children
- Funding research into eye diseases and treatment at the Department of Ophthalmology, University of Leicester
- The Ulverscroft Vision Research Group, Institute of Child Health
- Twin operating theatres at the Western Ophthalmic Hospital, London
- The Chair of Ophthalmology at the Royal Australian College of Ophthalmologists

You can help further the work of the Foundation
by making a donation or leaving a legacy.
Every contribution is gratefully received. If you
would like to help support the Foundation or
require further information, please contact:

THE ULVERSCROFT FOUNDATION
The Green, Bradgate Road, Anstey
Leicester LE7 7FU, England
Tel: (0116) 236 4325

website: www.foundation.ulverscroft.com

DREAMS OF YESTERDAY

On the eve of World War Two, Charlotte Moore is busy helping at her father's garage. There never seems to be an opportunity to have a bit of fun or a night out — until she attracts the attention of Robert Costello. But when he and her other friends and family go away to fight in the war, Charlotte is left in charge of the family business, as well as with constant worry. Will her loved ones come back alive?

JILL BARRY

◆

DREAMS OF YESTERDAY

Complete and Unabridged

17/2/2018

LINFORD
Leicester

First published in Great Britain in 2013

First Linford Edition
published 2014

Copyright © 2013 by Jill Barry
All rights reserved

A catalogue record for this book is available
from the British Library.

ISBN 978–1–4448–1970–0

Published by
F. A. Thorpe (Publishing)
Anstey, Leicestershire

Set by Words & Graphics Ltd.
Anstey, Leicestershire
Printed and bound in Great Britain by
T. J. International Ltd., Padstow, Cornwall

This book is printed on acid-free paper

If you really want to,
you should take the chance.

The Flying Circus

Charlotte craned her neck, determined not to lose sight of the tiny speck she'd watched take off minutes before. In the distance the fragile aeroplane banked steeply above the shimmering sea before heading back to the field. The plane loomed larger, its boxy wings looking fit to snap clean in half, like a biscuit.

But Charlotte's visits to the field where the flying circus had thrilled fans for the last few days told her the small craft was in expert hands. She held her breath as the plane lost height, its nose pointing towards the grass landing strip. The mix of showmanship and judgement on the pilot's part produced a lump in her throat as the plane's tyres kissed the ground.

'Are you waiting to have a go, Charlotte?'

She whirled around. Suddenly she felt shy and her heart seemed to beat a little faster. Robert Costello was a couple of years her senior and only recently had she begun to think of him as someone other than one of those bothersome boys her older brother knocked about with. Annoyingly, she felt warmth flood her cheeks, a warmth having nothing to do with the August sunshine bathing the countryside.

'I don't think so, Robert. Dad would probably have me hung, drawn and quartered!'

Robert laughed. 'I reckon you'd have to land in one piece before he could arrange that. How anyone can trust those flimsy things beats me.'

'They're sturdier than they look.'

'You're an expert then?'

She knew he was teasing. Probably he still thought of her as a fourteen-year-old in ankle socks.

'You know very well I'm not,' she said. 'It's just that . . .'

'Just that you've watched this particular pilot lots of times?' His eyes were curious.

'How did you know that? I mean, why would you think that?' Light dawned. 'Ah, Don's been talking.'

'This has nothing to do with your brother. That fancy fly-boy over there came to watch the Wall of Death last night. He and his mechanic were boasting about all the pretty girls flocking to take a pleasure flight.' Robert squared his shoulders. 'I told him the Wall of Death riders attract their fair share of admiration from girls.'

'Well, here's one girl who hasn't flown with Philip.' She bit her lip, cross with herself for letting slip the pilot's name.

Robert looked at her quizzically. 'First name terms is it? I didn't know you were such a fast worker. I expect he likes blondes . . . oh, there's some beetroot cheeks for you.'

Charlotte drew herself up to her full height. 'It's none of your business who

3

I'm on first name terms with, Mr Costello.'

'Ouch! All right, Miss Moore, let's call a truce.' He nodded towards the little aircraft taxiing over the bumpy ground towards the big sign proclaiming Pleasure Flights. 'But don't go losing your heart to someone who won't take good care of it. I'd hate to see you hurt.' He looked at his watch. 'I'd offer you a lift but I see you're driving Daddy's Vauxhall.'

The words were spoken with resignation rather than envy. She watched Robert walk off towards the cluster of vehicles parked near the gate. When she turned her attention back to the flying circus crew, Philip the pilot, leather jacket unbuttoned, white silk scarf fluttering in the breeze, was signing autograph books for three or four girls, the friend who'd accompanied her among them.

Charlotte saw Philip treat Pearl to a full-beam smile and shook her head ruefully. The pilot must have made a big hit with her. Maybe Pearl was the one Robert Costello should warn not to fall in love with someone unattainable. It certainly puzzled Charlotte as to why Robert cared whether her own heart got broken or not.

She strolled towards the entrance to the roped area. As she approached the group, the darkly handsome aviator glanced up and smiled.

'Good afternoon, Charlie. Changed your mind about taking to the skies?'

'I'm afraid not, Philip. I must get back so Dad can have his tea. Ready, Pearl?'

Her friend nodded, hands clutching a red suede autograph book as if she might tuck it beneath her pillow when she went to bed that night.

Philip stood, hands on leather-clad hips. 'It's been a pleasure to talk to you, Pearl. I'll call at the garage to say goodbye before we leave town, Charlie. I've enjoyed your dad's company the times we've talked engines.' He hesitated. 'And yours, of course.'

'Two more for you, Phil,' called the mechanic. 'Last trip today.'

The pilot gazed at Charlotte. 'Sure you won't hang on till I finish? I could take you and your friend here up for a short flight.'

Charlotte heard Pearl's surprised gasp but wasn't about to trample all over her dad's wishes. Despite his love of engines, he shared Robert Costello's wary opinion about aviation.

'Thanks, Philip. You're very kind but I must get back. I'll see you soon, then.' She turned to Pearl. 'Ready?'

Charlotte rummaged in her handbag for the car key as she and Pearl walked back to the parking area.

'I wish we could've gone up,' said Pearl longingly.

'I thought I heard you say on the way here, you'd probably be sick if you got airborne?'

'That was before I met Philip,' said Pearl. 'How come I haven't seen him when he's called at your dad's garage? Have you been hiding him from me?'

'When you've been working in the office, he's been in the workshop with

6

my father,' said Charlotte. 'I got enough teasing from Robert just now without you starting. I'd be crazy to want such a daredevil for a boyfriend and so would you.'

She shot her friend a quick glance as they arrived at the car. Charlotte went round to the passenger door to unlock it and Pearl stepped daintily over the running board and settled into the leather bucket seat.

'Why do you think Robert was teasing you?' Pearl pulled the door closed with a clunk.

Charlotte already sat behind the steering wheel. 'Because he enjoys ruffling my feathers? Because he seems to think I don't have a mind of my own?' She started the engine.

'But you like him all right, don't you?'

Charlotte tucked her dark green cotton skirt around her legs as she selected reverse gear.

'Who?'

'Why, Robert, of course!'

Pearl received no answer.

7

The Girl on the Pumps

'There you are, Charlotte. My stomach's beginning to wonder if my throat's been cut.'

'Sorry, Dad. I dropped Pearl off on the way back because her shoes were pinching, then I had to change. There's a ham salad on the table all ready for you — potatoes in the pan on the stove.'

'Thanks, love. I won't be long putting that away. You might get Mr Graham call on his way back from work. His spare tyre's mended and the bill's written out ready.' Mr Moore scratched his head. 'Blimey, I almost forgot. Your brother's gone to Browns to collect some parts needed for tomorrow. Oh, and Pump Number Three's out of action. I've put a padlock on.'

'Dad, you don't want to miss the five o'clock news. I'll be fine.'

'You always are, love.' Her father hurried towards the entrance leading to the family's house.

Left alone, Charlotte walked on to the forecourt. As usual, everything looked tidy, petrol pipes looped neatly and airline hose coiled inside its little wooden box ready for the next customer. The curls of black rubber tubing reminded her of a Catherine Wheel, or the liquorice sweet her dad always picked first from the pack if they opened a bag of Allsorts.

She stood in the evening sunshine, trim in her dungarees, thinking how much she liked working for the family business. The garage had occupied this spot since the 1920s when her dad, helped by his father, had scraped together the purchase price to obtain the land. Charlotte wasn't old enough to remember the construction. During that time, she, her brother and her mum and dad were all still living with an elderly aunt, a widow with a house she'd told them made her feel like a pea rattling around in a pan before they moved in.

Charlotte waved as a double-decker bus trundled past, the driver giving her a cheery salute as he slowed his cumbersome vehicle ready to pull up at the nearby stop. The Corner Garage lent its name to the stop and some passengers had been using that same local bus service for years. The vehicle following the bus was a small black car driven by the customer Charlotte awaited.

She disappeared inside and reappeared, rolling a tyre along the ground. The customer pulled up outside the workshop entrance and jumped out. 'How's my favourite girl, then?'

'She's not here, Mr Graham. I'm afraid you'll have to make do with me.' Charlotte grinned at him.

He laughed as he opened his boot. 'You'll make some lucky fellow very happy one day, Charlie. Prince Charming hasn't come along yet, by any chance?'

She shook her head. 'I don't think petrol makes a very good perfume, Mr Graham. And boys don't like it when they find out I know more about engines than they do.'

Mr Graham followed her into the office, to settle his bill. He looked shrewdly at her as she slipped behind the counter.

'Then all I can say is, they must have a screw loose. You have to be the prettiest girl in Peel Bay. My wife said she saw you in the high street the other day and got quite a shock. Young Charlie's turned into a beauty, she said.'

'Gosh,' said Charlotte. 'I don't think Mrs Graham would say the same thing if she saw me in my dungarees and lace-up shoes.' She grimaced and took the big white five-pound note Mr Graham held out to her.

'All the fine clothes in the world can't disguise a plain face. Mark my words, Charlie, some young fellow's going to pull up here for a gallon of petrol one day, take one look at those sparkling brown eyes of yours and be putty in your hands.'

Smiling, she handed over the change. 'Better not tell my dad you're trying to marry off his right-hand woman.'

Her cheerful tone didn't disguise the seriousness underlying the remark. Charlotte had lost her mother three years before.

'Your father thinks the world of you all right.' Mr Graham pocketed his change. 'But you deserve a bit of fun. I bet your mother would say the same, God rest her soul . . . ' His voice tailed away and he bit his lip.

'Well, who's to say whether any of us will have time for fun unless things change dramatically?' Charlotte picked up a duster and gave the counter top such a vigorous rub, the dust motes danced a jig in the shaft of sunshine beaming through the window.

'It's not looking good,' he said. 'Not good at all. But don't forget what I say.'

Charlotte walked the customer back

to his car and watched him drive off just as her brother turned up, driving their little blue van, its white lettering stating *Corner Garage* and *Peel Bay 642* telephone number on the sides. He drove into the workshop and parked.

Donald Moore's lanky frame unravelled itself from the front seat while Charlotte unfastened the rear doors to see what was inside.

'Don't go lifting those boxes, our kid,' said Don, arriving beside his sister. 'They can stay inside the van 'til tomorrow.'

'Why so chivalrous all of a sudden?'

He grinned. 'Kitty's influence I expect. She keeps telling me I should be nicer to my little sister.'

'She's quite right. Are you seeing her this evening?'

'Would I waste a precious night off? I'm taking her to the flicks.'

'Which one?'

'The Carlton's showing *A Yank at Oxford*.

'Pearl said *Angels with Dirty Faces* is

13

on at The Capitol.'

'That means driving to Coynesbury. D'you think Kitty would like a gangster film?'

'How should I know?'

'You're a girl. Do girls like films about gangsters?'

'Pearl and I do. Are you scared Kitty might faint?'

'All right, all right. She can decide.'

'You'd better get a move on. Dad's eating his tea and yours is waiting.' She gave him a friendly shove. 'Don't forget to have a good wash. You've got oil on your left ear lobe.'

'What would we do without you, little sister?'

'You'd have to manage, wouldn't you?'

As her brother hurried off to the house, Charlotte wondered how she and her dad would cope when war was declared and Don had to go away to fight. A shiver rippled down her spine. Far better she concentrated on count- ing the day's takings and leaving a sensible float for the morning. On a fine evening like this, her father would probably remain open until nine o'clock. If she remained on duty with him, she'd be lucky to sit down with her library book for half an hour before bedtime.

She'd almost forgotten what it was like to look forward to an evening out. It wouldn't just involve putting on a crisp cotton frock instead of her practical dungarees. A night out would mean applying her English Rose lipstick and a dab of gardenia cologne behind each ear. She wondered what it would be like to sit in the stalls, holding hands with a young man. Had she become too serious, too intent on making a good job of her domestic role as well as helping out in the garage? Was that what Mr Graham meant when he told her she deserved a bit of fun?

The sound of a horn tooting roused Charlotte. She hurried on to the forecourt where a big black Daimler stood. Her heart sank. Stanley Greener was one of her dad's best customers. She'd better stop daydreaming and serve him with his usual four gallons of best petrol. Mr Greener, perspiring as usual, clambered out of the driver's seat, ready to engage her in pointless conversation. She prayed her father would finish his tea soon.

Just as she was wondering how Mrs Greener tolerated her husband's highly scented and extremely greasy hair cream, a couple of lads came round the corner. One of them carried an empty jerry can, which he placed on the ground. The youngsters stood, chattering and scuffling while Charlotte served Mr Greener with petrol.

'I shan't be long, boys. Paraffin for your mum is it, Jack?'

Jack wiped his nose on his sleeve. 'Yes, please, Miss. Hey Mister, I like your car.'

Mr Greener looked slightly mollified. 'Thanks, son. Do you want a look inside?'

Charlotte restrained from giggling as

the boys kept her customer busy with question after question. Everyone knew Mr Greener considered himself as a ladies' man and the arrival of this pair of lads saved her from having to put up with inane comments from the smarmy so and so!

She watched the dial as the hands moved towards the four gallon mark, released the pressure on the trigger and allowed the last few drops of fuel to dribble into the tank. Mr Greener was still boasting to the boys so Charlotte hurried into the office and riffled through the customer accounts box to find the card she needed. Taking it out to the forecourt would hasten his departure.

Guiltily she pulled a duster from her pocket and gave his windscreen a quick polish as he signed for his fuel. The boys watched him drive away.

The elder looked at Charlotte. 'D'you think I'll own a car like that one day, Miss?'

She smiled at him. 'I don't see why

not, Jack. You'll need to work very hard at school, though.'

'If the war's still on when I'm eighteen, I'll have to go and fight the Germans, won't I? I bet I'd kill dozens and dozens.'

Jack's pal made machine gun noises, his face contorting, his hands clutching an imaginary rifle. Charlotte bit her lip, suddenly sad that these two, and countless like them, lived under a dark cloud. 'Let's hope things work out so that's not necessary, boys,' she said.

Bright Lights and Shadows

Charlotte pulled the grill pan away from the flames just in time. Even so, the bread crusts already resembled strips of charcoal.

'Burnt offerings is it, ducks?' Don came into the kitchen and pulled out a chair. 'Aw, don't look like that. You know I didn't mean it.'

'Mum would never have dished up cheese on toast like this.' Charlotte looked down gloomily at the two plates as she took her place at the table.

Don reached for the bottle of brown sauce. 'Our mother wasn't trying to do two different jobs,' he said gently.

Charlotte stared at him. 'That never occurred to me. Why are you being so nice to me, big brother?'

He chewed steadily, waving his fork

at her. 'We're a team. We have to be. The way things are going, we'll have worse things to fight than our sisters and brothers.'

She sipped at her glass of water, remembering Jack's earnest round face. 'I keep trying not to think about it but it's not going to go away, is it?'

'No, it's not. What worries me most is Dad's attitude.'

'I don't understand.' Charlotte frowned. 'What's he been saying?'

'If war's declared, he wants to join up again.'

'I hope to goodness you're joking.'

Don bit into a crust and crunched it between his teeth. 'I like this burnt flavour,' he said when he could.

'Don't change the subject. How can Dad possibly want to do that? Surely he's too old?'

'For active service he is. He did his bit in the last war. But with his experience of motor vehicles, he could volunteer for other duties.'

'What about the business? If you go

and he goes, the Corner Garage would have to finish trading. He wouldn't let that happen, surely?'

Don shrugged. 'These are changing times, Charlie. Please don't say anything to him. I know for sure he won't want you worrying about it.'

'Because I'm a girl, you mean?' She pursed her lips.

'Because you're his daughter, you knucklehead. You've gone through enough without having to face up to a war.'

Charlotte pushed her plate away.

'Aren't you going to finish your tea?'

'You can have it if you like,' she said. 'Then, if you go and relieve Dad, I'll try and make his without burning it to a crisp.'

'Good girl. Why don't you take yourself off somewhere this evening? Go and call for Pearl and see if she fancies a walk.'

'I might take myself for a walk. This is Pearl's hair washing night.'

'Isn't that what girls do when they

need an excuse to turn down a date?'

His sister raised her eyebrows. 'Don't tell me you've had that happen to you.'

He shrugged. 'Not yet but to tell the truth, I'm not at all sure about Kitty's feelings. Maybe she's worried that I have to get dirty to make a living. When we went to the pictures, she said she was embarrassed because she could smell petrol on me. I do my best to scrub up. You know I do.'

Charlotte concentrated on slicing two perfect rounds of white bread. 'When are you seeing her next?'

'Saturday afternoon. There's a tea dance at Randalls. Kitty likes putting on her glad rags.' He rose and carried both dirty plates over to the draining board. 'I'll buy you a bar of that milk chocolate you like if you make a good job of ironing my best shirt.' He leaned against the sink, arms folded.

'You could have a bath before you eat your dinner on Saturday. That should make sure you smell sweet enough to escort your girl friend to the swankiest

22

place in Peel Bay. How's that for an idea?'

'You're on. Shall I tell Dad his tea's ready?'

'It'll be about five minutes.'

'And afterwards you'll get out of the house and stop worrying?'

'I'll go for a walk but I can't guarantee to stop worrying.'

Don nodded. 'Why don't you go down to the prom? Most of the day trippers will have left by the time you get there.'

'Won't there be lots of courting couples on a lovely evening like this? I might feel like I'm a gooseberry.'

He shuffled his feet and examined his fingernails. 'You know, Charlie, it wouldn't be the end of the world if you found a boyfriend.'

She raised her eyes heavenwards. 'Not you as well. Has Mr Graham been saying something?'

'Mr Graham who drives the black Austin? Hardly! Should he have?'

She turned her back and slid the grill

23

pan under the flames. 'Go and call Dad. I shan't move from this spot until his tea's tastier than they'd serve at a Lyons' Corner House.'

*　*　*

Charlotte strolled down the quiet residential street and crossed over at the bottom, heading along the old harbour. A few people walked ahead of her and she overtook a girl she'd known at school, walking with her younger sister. Charlotte called a greeting as she passed, striding along with purpose, not wanting to be drawn into conversation. A tiny breeze ruffled her golden curls as she stopped on the promenade, leaned her elbows on top of the wall and gazed at the sea.

A broad-bottomed paddle steamer, returning from an excursion, cruised through the calm waters towards the pier. Charlotte could make out the passengers on deck. One or two waved and she returned the greeting. A small craft from the yachting club kept well away from the choppy water in the steamer's wake, unlike the gang of greedy seagulls, homing in and squabbling over any leftovers suitable for their supper.

The cool evening air made Charlotte glad of the white angora bolero she wore over her red and white spotted dress. She hadn't been sure what to change into after she finished washing up the tea things. Hadn't really been sure what she expected from this precious evening on her own. A summer dress and sandals were a very different look from dungarees and sensible shoes. She'd drawn the line at the lipstick and dab of scent though. It seemed like a fast thing to do when she was only taking a walk. That was probably what her mum would have thought.

Charlotte set off again, walking towards Fun Land, anticipation causing her heart to beat that little bit faster, the colourful lights and jaunty music of the Dutch barrel organ making her feet want to tap.

The small pleasure park, owned by Robert Costello's father, provided employment for a couple of dozen men who were either Peel Bay residents or itinerant workers, putting down temporary roots for the summer season. The stallholders paid for their pitches and offered a variety of games, all with prizes propped on shelves, to tempt visitors to part with their money.

For the last two years, the Wall of Death had been pulling in good crowds. Charlotte was well aware her father wouldn't approve of her hanging around 'that place' as he described it. But the pungent hot smell of grease and the roar of the engines drew her like a powerful magnet attracting a pin.

A loudspeaker announcement told her the riders were about to commence the next display. Charlotte hesitated. Should she, shouldn't she? Out of the corner of her eye, she noticed a couple of flashily dressed men looking over at her. One of them muttered something to the other and began moving in her direction. What should she do? She clutched her handbag to her chest, feet frozen to the ground. Was she totally crazy, coming over to Fun Land on her own in the evening, even though it was still broad daylight? Don should have known better than to encourage her. Yet it had seemed such a good idea at the time.

She looked the other way but when a hand cupped her elbow, she whirled round, determined not to show her fear. Relief flooded her at the sight of Robert Costello, dressed in a pair of blue overalls, his eyes for some unknown reason expressing an amazing amount of concern.

'Charlotte! You're not on your own, surely?'

'There's no law against it, is there?'

When he smiled, she liked the way his eyes crinkled. And those eyes were an extraordinary shade of green. Why had she never noticed that before?

27

'You're quite entitled to be here,' said Robert. 'I was surprised to see you turn up without a friend in tow, that's all.'

'I don't have that many friends, Robert.' She startled herself by blurting out the comment.

'Well, that's something we have in common,' he said.

'You and me both work odd hours,' said Charlotte, on the defensive. 'When you're involved in running the family business, it makes it difficult to do ordinary things.'

'Like going to the pictures,' he said.

'Nor do we know the meaning of nine to five,' she said, still looking into those green, green eyes.

'How right you are.'

'I don't usually go out of an evening,' said Charlotte.

'So this is your night off and you're spending it on your own?'

She nodded. 'Don and my father are on duty.'

'I bet you cooked their tea and washed up before coming out?'

28

'Of course,' she said. 'And made ham sandwiches for them to eat when they close the garage.'

Robert swallowed hard. 'I don't suppose . . . I mean, unless you desperately want to watch the Wall of Death . . . could I maybe buy you a cup of coffee?'

Her eyes flickered over his oil-stained overalls. Maybe he intended taking her to a refreshment kiosk. 'That would be very nice,' she said.

'I'm not quite off duty but I think I can twist my father's arm.' He smiled down at her. 'Meet you in the Velvet Ice-cream Parlour ten minutes from now? I need to clean up a bit first.'

'Really?' Charlotte's eyes danced.

'Yes, really.' He smiled at her then looked around. 'I'd prefer you to wait for me somewhere safe. Come to think of it, how about you stay by the ticket office? The lady on duty will keep an eye on you.'

'Thank you but I'm not a child, Robert.'

'I'm very aware of that, Charlotte,' he said. 'Come on. As soon as I've made myself respectable, I'll collect you. You can have a peep at the show while you wait. If anyone says anything, just you tell them the boss' son said it was all right.'

*　　*　　*

The Velvet Ice Cream Parlour overlooked the promenade. Its silver and black Art Deco sleekness made it a popular venue not only for day-trippers and holidaymakers but for the town's residents as well. Charlie had always loved being brought there by her mother and treasured fond memories of being allowed to choose a Knickerbocker Glory on her twelfth birthday when she'd been deemed tall enough to see over the tall glass and dip the long-handled spoon into the delicious concoction of fruit, nuts and ice cream.

'So what did you think of the riders?' Robert sat back in his green wicker chair and looked expectantly at her.

Charlie swirled her spoon in the raspberry sauce topping her double vanilla ice-cream wafer. 'I thought the Wall was thrilling. I like speed.'

'I suppose that's why the flying circus attracts you? Or, maybe it's one of the reasons.' His lips set in a thin line.

She shrugged, ignoring the innuendo. 'I hadn't really thought about it. The Wall of Death and the Flying Circus are both daredevil things, aren't they? It's odd you're mad about motorbikes yet you seem dead set against flying. Why do you think that is?'

He stirred sugar into his coffee. 'It's not so far to fall if you're a Wall of Death rider.'

'Have you ever had a go? On the Wall, I mean?'

He shook his head. 'Even if I wanted to, I couldn't spare the time. The boys are the experts and there are a million and one things to do around Fun Land. Joe Muggins here usually gets lumbered with most of them.'

'I know how you feel.' She ate a spoonful of ice cream. 'Do you mind if I ask you something, Robert?'

'Fire away,' he said.

'Did you know I was coming here this evening?'

He shook his head. 'Certainly not. I had quite a surprise. A pleasant one though.' He smiled at her uncertainly then looked down at his cup.

'I got a surprise too, seeing you at the flying circus the other afternoon,' said Charlie.

She watched in amazement as his cheeks reddened.

'Are you sweet on Pearl? Did Don tell you she'd asked if she could come with me? Was that why you turned up?'

He drained his cup. 'What a lot of questions. I'm sure I don't know what you mean! Come on. I'll give you a lift home on my bike. We need to leave now so I can be back to help Dad close.'

'I can walk home, Robert. It won't be dark for ages yet.'

He stood up. 'Why do women always have to argue?'

She looked after him as he approached the counter to pay the bill. Suddenly and inexplicably she couldn't bear the thought of him being sweet on Pearl. But he obviously didn't want to talk about the subject and she daren't probe further. After all, it was none of her business.

They left the ice cream parlour in silence. Strings of coloured lights outlined the rides still open. Other pitches stood in darkness, their waterproof covers transforming them into bulky, sinister shadows. As Charlotte and Robert walked towards the Wall of Death, she saw the lights on the Cakewalk extinguish as if a giant hand snuffed them one by one. In the nearby arcade of amusement machines, hopeful punters pushed pennies into slots or rolled coins down wooden chutes. The mechanical laughing policeman's manic chuckle sounded menacing. Charlotte shivered.

When Robert's arm moved protectively around her waist, it seemed the most natural thing in the world to lean in to him. Yet, she had to know.

'You didn't answer me when I asked you about Pearl.'

Robert chuckled. 'You are the most amazing and annoying girl in the world, Charlotte Moore. Do you know that?'

'Well, I do now, Robert Costello. And I'm still waiting for an answer.'

'Heavens above, do I have to spell it out for you? Not that it would do me much good, I reckon.'

When he removed his arm from her waist she missed its comforting presence.

'What are you trying to say?' She pulled a pale grey headscarf from her handbag as he sat astride his motorbike.

He looked at her as she knotted the scarf under her chin. 'Hop on,' he said. 'Don't forget to hold tight.'

Robert accelerated away from the fun fair, Charlotte's arms wrapped round his waist while she wondered in her turn whether he was the most infuriating person she'd ever met. Two could play at that game. Yet, in spite of the chilly air rushing past, there was a warm feeling inside her she knew hadn't existed before he'd rescued her from what could have been an awkward situation. They cruised through the quiet streets and it seemed no time at all before he pulled into the kerb beside her front door and she clambered reluctantly from the pillion seat.

'Thanks for the lift home,' she said.

'Can I see you again, Charlotte?' Robert kept the engine idling, his goggles pushed up on his forehead.

'I don't understand. You know where I am.'

He threw back his head and laughed. 'Well, I wish I knew where I was,' he said. 'I mean I'd like us to go out together soon.'

'Go out?'

He sighed. 'Yes, as in boy and girl going out.'

Charlie's mouth was a round O of surprise. 'Without Donald or Pearl or anybody else being there?'

'That's the general idea. Look, I'd better get back or the old man will be on the warpath. Tell you what, I'll ring you and see if we can arrange to take the same night off. That would be a start. Cheerio . . . '

She stood, staring after him as he roared off.

The front door burst open and Mr Moore appeared on the scrubbed step. 'Oh, good, it's you, love,' he said. 'Get a lift back, did you? I've just made a pot of tea.'

'Robert Costello brought me home on his motorbike,' said Charlotte cautiously.

'I thought as much soon as I heard that engine. I hope he drove carefully.'

'Yes. Actually, I enjoyed riding pillion.' She lifted her chin, prepared for a lecture but her dad didn't comment.

'Let's sit down. Don's in the kitchen but I'm afraid he's not too chipper.'

She followed her dad through the hallway. Her brother sat at the kitchen table, his head in his hands.

'Don? Whatever is it? Are you ill?' Charlotte rushed to his side and dropped to her knees, everything else forgotten in her anxiety.

He sat up and rubbed the back of his neck. 'Don't fuss, Charlie. I'm afraid she's given me my marching orders. Made a proper chump of me, she has.'

For a moment Charlotte couldn't think what he meant. Then it dawned on her. 'You mean Kitty?'

'Who else? She's decided she doesn't want to be tied down. Says she's too young to go steady. It's an excuse of course. She's nearly nineteen, for goodness' sake.'

His sister got up to fetch the milk jug. 'You could do with a nice, hot cuppa. Dad will pour the tea while I find some biscuits.'

The men were silent, making Charlotte aware how much she'd sounded like her mum. She undid the wrapping on a packet of ginger nuts and the little family sat around the table in silence.

'Worse things happen at sea, lad,' said Mr Moore.

Don did his best to smile though it turned out lop-sided. 'This has knocked me off my perch,' he said. 'It'll be a while before I ask another girl to go out with me, that's for sure.'

Charlotte bit her lip. Her heart seemed to have soared with the birds this evening and now it had plummeted to earth in tune with her brother's bitterness. How could she talk about Robert's invitation and quiz Don about his possible involvement when her brother obviously felt so low?

'But you were going to take her to Randalls on Saturday,' she said. 'The Tea Dance sounded a lovely idea. Did she come here to tell you she'd changed her mind?'

He fidgeted with his teaspoon. 'She sent her little brother round with a note. The kid left it on the office counter then I saw him scarper while I was checking a customer's oil level.'

'What a rotten thing to do, sending her little brother to do her dirty work.' Charlotte's cheeks flushed in anger. 'I'd never have believed Kitty was such a fly-by-night! She seemed such a nice girl. Why, if Mum was here now she'd be round her house, giving the baggage a piece of her mind!'

Donald shrugged, his eyes begging Charlotte not to bring back painful memories.

Mr Moore stirred his tea, breaking the silence. 'All right, love. We're all upset. I'm sorry to have to say it, Don, but maybe it's for the best. The news doesn't get any better. I think there's no escaping another war, I really do. I've kept hoping for the situation to improve but my guess is it won't be long before Germany lays its cards on the table. Upheaval all over again — that's what we're in for, son. And the likes of us can't do a thing about it.'

Charlotte closed her eyes in a brief prayer. Please don't let anything happen

Charlotte Makes Progress

Over the next few days, Charlotte alternated between waiting for Robert to ring and worrying about Don. She deliberately put out of her mind all thoughts of the looming thunderclouds, sensibly deciding, as her dad reckoned, there was nothing anyone could do about it so why waste time mooning around the place?

The fourth morning after her night out, she made her usual progress to the high street. A friend of the family ran the greengrocery and Charlie enjoyed calling in for a chat and placing an order which was always delivered within a few hours.

'This season's Victorias are in, Charlotte,' called the proprietress as the shop bell pinged.

Charlie stepped inside the shop. 'Dad and Don will be pleased, Maggie.'

Charlie peered at the fragrant pile of purple fruit.

'Try one. Sweet as honey they are.'

'I won't say no.' Charlie bit into the firm, ripe plum. 'Whoops! Trust me to dribble juice down my chin. But they're lovely and I'll have a pound, please.'

'Got your list ready?'

Charlie blinked hard. 'Goodness, I must be getting absent-minded. I clean forgot to make one today.'

'Sounds like you're in love.'

Charlotte stared at her, the flippant remark hitting home, especially as she normally organised her shopping very well.

'Don't worry.' Maggie picked up a notepad and pencil. 'Just shout out what you want.'

When another customer arrived, Charlie took the paper and pencil and finished writing down the remaining items she required. As soon as the customer left, Maggie leaned across the counter. 'Have you heard about Fun Land?'

'Heard what about Fun Land?' Charlie tucked a strand of hair behind her ear.

'You really should get your god-mother to give you a trim, love. As for Fun Land, the Costellos have decided to close down early this season.' Maggie lowered her voice although the two of them were still on their own. 'I've heard a rumour they mightn't ever open again.'

Charlie ignored the comment about her unruly hair. 'This is news to me. Dad usually gets to hear about things happening in Peel Bay but I can't understand why Robert's said nothing to . . . um, to Don,' she added hastily.

'I know those two are pals but maybe Robert was too embarrassed to mention it. It's not easy for businesses like Fun Land to keep going. Everything's up in the air and I don't mean the flying circus.'

Charlie sighed. Maybe this was why Robert hadn't been in touch. He had more important things on his mind.

'Sometimes,' she said, 'I wish the flipping war would get going so we all knew where we were.'

Maggie sucked in her breath. 'Don't say that, my girl. You weren't born when the first one changed our lives and took away our sweethearts. At least dear Noelene got your dad back safe and sound. Some of us weren't so lucky. Not a day goes by without I don't think of my late husband.'

Charlie was round the counter in a flash. She put her arms round the older woman. 'I'm so sorry. That was a stupid, thoughtless remark. I could kick myself.' In her mind's eye she saw Don and Robert's faces, sometimes intent as they bent over a carburettor but usually smiling as they joshed one another, arguing amiably about football. Lately though, neither had been exactly sunshine and roses. Her brother must be still smarting after Kitty's casual treatment and as for Robert, he was such an unknown quantity.

44

Another possibility struck her. Perhaps he hadn't been in touch because of Don's broken romance. Perhaps he was having second thoughts, in case he should suffer the same fate. If only she could make him aware how swiftly her feelings towards him had softened and deepened.

Maggie took out a handkerchief and blew her nose loudly. 'I'm a silly old woman with too many memories,' she said. 'You young ones have to stay strong and pray for right to triumph.' She put away her hanky. 'We'll have your order round to you by lunchtime, as usual. Don't forget what I said about your crowning glory. We wouldn't want Eleanor to run out of business, now would we? Strikes me, it's more important than ever for us tradesmen to support each other.'

★　★　★

The news of the Costello predicament stayed with Charlotte, dropping into

45

her mind as she called in at one of the two butcher's shops her family favoured. She also visited the biggest grocery on the high street, the one her mum had always used. She squeezed between a sack of red lentils and one of gleaming pearl barley to queue at the counter then ask for a couple of items she'd almost run out of. As she put a packet of tea and a bag of sugar into her shopping basket she realised her library book still sat at the bottom of the basket and carefully retrieved it, ready to take back to the tuppenny library.

The bookshelves at the tobacconist's shop were situated in a small room at the back. This was where, if time permitted, Charlotte loved to linger longest. She'd inherited a love of reading from her mother, and while her mum had favoured stories of desert sheikhs and square-jawed doctors, much to her parents' amazement Charlotte preferred adventure stories aimed more at boys than girls. But today she found herself drawn to the romantic novels. She felt a twinge of nostalgia as she picked out one whose cover showed a pretty brunette dressed in nurse's uniform, complete with snowy pleated cap, certain her mother had read and enjoyed this story in the past.

Breathing in the smell of tobacco and books, she flicked through the first pages. The hero seemed to be giving the heroine a hard time. Huh! Charlie could identify with that. Maybe she'd learn a few tips about dealing with men. Brothers and fathers didn't count — probably her dad and Don would be horrified if they knew she contemplated contacting Robert, even though he'd said he would telephone her to try and arrange a meeting. That would not be considered something a nice girl would do.

The tobacconist smiled at Charlotte and wrote the book title on her library card. She'd swapped *Tales of the Gold Monkey* for *The Dawn*. Maybe reading how the heroine dealt with her handsome Arab sheikh would throw some light on her own jumbled emotions. There were so many things she wished she'd spoken to her mum about and somehow, deciding to read the kind of book she would have chosen brought Noelene that little bit closer to Charlotte. Running an amusement park mightn't be something an Arab sheikh would know about but sharing in someone else's romantic trials and tribulations would help Charlie better understand her own feelings.

When she stepped into the street again, she decided to call at her godmother's salon and book an appointment. Maggie's blunt comment had been accurate. Charlie's hair, left to its own devices, resembled a golden dandelion clock and wasn't a sensible option, given the rain and wind she often endured when serving customers.

As it happened, Auntie Eleanor could fit Charlie in straight after lunch. If she hurried back, she could prepare the men's meals while eating a snack as she worked. Having her hair done was a rare occurrence and, grudgingly, she thought it might add to her confidence when she plucked up courage to go and speak to Robert. She closed the salon door behind her and set off in the direction of home, the romantic novel perched on top of her shopping.

'Hey, what's your hurry?'

Charlie stopped and grinned at Philip the pilot. 'Fancy seeing you. I can't stop, I'm afraid. There's the meal to get then I'm back for a hairdo.'

'What a shame. I'm kicking my heels today. Gerald's taking the old kite apart and putting it together again.'

'Walk back with me if you like. We might even run to a bit of dinner for you if you don't mind cold meat and bubble and squeak.'

His face brightened. 'That sounds great. Thank you, Charlie.'

'When are you off?'

He took her shopping bag from her. 'As soon as Gerald's certain we're airworthy. It's Brighton next stop and I can't wait. Lots of pretty girls in Brighton.' He glanced sideways at her. 'But I'll miss you very much, of course.'

She laughed. 'Of course you will. By the way, Pearl's at the garage today — you'll find her in the office if you want to say ta-ta.'

'Pearl? Have I met her?'

Charlie stopped walking. 'You signed her autograph book not long ago. She thought you were lovely. I of course know different.'

Philip put his arm round her waist and gave her a quick squeeze just as Robert Costello rode past them on his motorbike. Charlie glanced up at the sound of his engine but too late to catch his eye or wave to him. Inwardly she groaned. This was typical of her luck. Robert disapproved of the flying circus and in particular of its star. In some ways Charlie found it easier to chat with Philip than with Robert, doubtless because how she felt about young Mr Costello differed entirely from the way she viewed Philip.

But if Robert had seen that quick hug, which seemed highly likely unless he drove with his eyes shut, would he decide she was too much of a flirt to waste his time upon? The sight of his ramrod straight back as he steered his machine up the high street stayed with Charlie and didn't improve her expectations of spending time with him and finding out what lay behind that sometimes secretive manner.

★   ★   ★

'We haven't seen you for a while, Charlotte.' Eleanor parted the cubicle's daisy-splashed curtains then pulled them closed behind her while her freckle-faced apprentice blotted surplus moisture from her client's forehead and neck.

Charlotte hated the whole process, including the uncomfortable crouch over the basin with the towel seemingly unable to prevent shampoo bubbles from stinging her eyes. 'You know me,

Auntie El. Mum used to chivvy me into coming. I don't mean to offend you but having my hair done isn't my favourite pastime.'

Eleanor laughed. 'I'd never have guessed! It's a good job all my clients aren't the same. Noelene used to love coming, of course.'

'Regular as clockwork, wasn't she? I must be a great disappointment to you.'

'Your mother's hair needed regular trimming. She used to like that bob style and it certainly suited her.'

'Dad used to call her his little flapper when he thought Don and I weren't listening.'

Eleanor hesitated. 'He must really miss her. You must all miss her, Charlie. I know that of course but they always seemed so close, those two. I can see so much of her in Donald, that glossy dark hair and straight nose. You're much more like your father.'

'You were at school with them, weren't you? I'd forgotten that.'

'I was in the same class as the

childhood sweethearts and I envied their closeness.'

Eleanor's eyes met Charlotte's in the mirror but she dropped her gaze and began combing perfumed setting lotion through her goddaughter's newly trimmed hair. Eleanor's junior stood ready, one large curler clutched in each hand. Charlotte reached up and wiped a drop of lotion from the end of her nose.

'Surely I don't need those instruments of torture! Couldn't you just dry my hair?'

Eleanor chuckled. 'If I use these big curlers then pop you under the dryer for half an hour the end result will be much smoother. Just you wait — you'll come out looking like Carole Lombard.'

'For about two minutes, maybe, then I'll be back to my Wild Woman of Borneo look. Go on then, you're the boss.'

'Usually I'd say the customer's always right, but in this case, I'm going to insist. You have lovely hair, Charlotte. Why not take advantage of it? Any signs of you courting yet?'

Charlotte heaved a sigh. 'No and it's unlikely there ever will be at this rate.'

'Why do you say that?' Eleanor twirled a thick strand of hair expertly around a blue curler and secured it with a giant hairpin.

'Men are just so difficult. They don't answer questions properly and they keep you dangling, knowing full well you can't make a move to speed things up. It's really annoying.'

She watched Eleanor smother a laugh. 'That's a bit harsh, isn't it?'

'I'm right though, aren't I?'

'I agree ladies aren't supposed to take the initiative. Would I happen to know the particular young man who's incurred your displeasure?'

Charlotte tipped her chin forward to allow Eleanor to roll the shorter hair at the nape of her neck. 'I doubt it,' she said. 'His parents run the amusement park.'

'Fun Land? Mrs Costello used to be one of my best clients. She liked her hair done regularly like your mother did but these days it's a different matter. I hear they're finding things difficult but then, so are many. Fun fairs are a luxury of course, when money's tight. I'm lucky to be in hairdressing.'

'Good job not all your clients are like me. But people like to let off steam if they're working hard. They want a bit of relaxation now and then. The Flying Circus has done well this week, I believe.'

'People know the plane's only there for a matter of days. They can pay their two shillings for a pleasure flight and have something to boast about. But the season will end soon. And then . . . '

'I know,' Charlotte butted in. 'And everything as we know it will probably change dramatically if there's a war. Already, I get a shivery feeling when I see sandbags being delivered. As for those awful gas masks . . . '

Eleanor concentrated upon the left

side of Charlotte's head, carefully teasing out the tangles. 'It's horrible to think of it happening all over again. But these precautions are necessary, Charlotte.' She combed out a strand and the apprentice passed her a chubby curler. 'Let's talk about more cheerful matters. Have you reached some kind of understanding with your young man?'

'Goodness, no! And he's definitely not my young man. We've not spent much time together at all. He did say he'd ring me to arrange for us to meet but now he's seen me talking to Philip the Pilot in the high street, he's probably gone right off me.' Charlotte tried to keep her tone light-hearted.

Eleanor frowned at the girl's reflection in the mirror. 'Surely not? You're a friendly sort of person, he must know that.'

'The trouble is, Philip put his arm around my waist at the very moment Robert drove past. If I'd been on my own, he might've stopped for a little chat.'

'I see. Well, maybe you could get Don

to have a word . . . oh, don't shake your head Charlie!'

'Sorry. I'd be far too embarrassed to ask Don. If Robert really wants to take me out, he should get in touch. He knows as well as I do the flying circus leaves town soon. Philip can't wait to get to Brighton. He's a shocking flirt, probably he's leaving broken hearts all over the south of England.'

Eleanor chuckled. 'He sounds quite a lad.'

She continued her task while Charlotte watched the hairdresser's nimble fingers fly. At last Eleanor pulled a net over Charlotte's head then patted her shoulder through the royal blue salon gown. 'You're ready to go under the hairdryer now. We'll find you a magazine and I'll be back later to comb you out. If I were you, I wouldn't waste your new hairdo. Ask your brother to take you down to the fair this evening if your dad doesn't need him. Robert Costello can't possibly ignore the sister of his best mate.'

Plain Speaking

'Hey.' Philip gave a low whistle of admiration. 'You look very glamorous, Charlie. I wish I could take you dancing.'

'It makes a change from my head-scarf and dungarees look, I suppose.' She turned to Pearl, seated at the back of the office. 'I hope this young gentleman hasn't been too much of an interruption for you. I did suggest he came to say hello.'

'He's been charming the lady customers,' said Pearl, 'as well as bending your dad's ear, of course. Your hair really does look lovely, Charlie.'

'I'm going to miss Raymond,' said Philip, looking pensive. 'He knows engines inside out and I respect him for that, even if he thinks aeroplanes are the devil's work.'

'Well, I expect both Dad and Don

will be looking for a cuppa. I'll go and make us all one, shall I?'

'I'll give you a hand,' offered Philip.

'I can manage quite well on my own. But if you come round to the house in about ten minutes, you can carry the tray through for me.'

'It's a deal. I was just about to ask Pearl here if she fancied a little jaunt to the pleasure park with you and me this evening.'

'You and me? First I heard of it.' But Charlotte's heart raced as fast as her mind worked out the possibilities. They were sure to see Robert. He'd take one look at Philip, who she could instruct to act as if he was smitten with Pearl, and surely then he'd realise Charlie herself had no interest whatsoever in the pilot.

'I'm game if you are, Charlie,' said Pearl, brightening.

'I suppose I should be doing the ironing but I can get up earlier tomorrow.'

'I'm flattered,' said Philip solemnly. 'To think you'd choose my company over that of an upstanding fellow like an ironing board makes me very happy, indeed.' He winked at Pearl.

'Looks like everyone's happy, then,' said Charlotte. 'After all, it's almost your last evening in Peel Bay so we ought to keep you company.'

Philip treated Pearl to a long, smouldering look. 'I'm only just beginning to realise what I'm leaving behind.'

Charlotte raised her eyes heavenwards, seeing Pearl's cheeks turn a delicate shade of pink. Hopefully her friend wouldn't let the pilot turn her head as easily. Once this evening was over, neither of them was likely to meet Philip ever again.

★   ★   ★

After tea, Charlie decided to change into the same dress she'd worn the evening she walked down to the promenade. Maybe it would bring her luck, especially if she dared to dab on some perfume as well. Pearl called for her, looking pretty in a cream blouse and yellow and cream skirt. Both girls wore lightweight summer sandals on their feet.

'It's a pity Don can't come,' said Charlie as the two of them set off.

'He looks a bit downcast lately,' said Pearl. 'I suppose he still holds a torch for Kitty.'

'I'm afraid so. No good telling him he's better off without her. I've tried that and got my head bitten off for my trouble.'

'He hardly ever takes any notice of me,' said Pearl, linking her arm in Charlie's as they waited to cross the road. 'I suppose that's one of the good things about Philip. He's very attentive.'

Charlotte decided not to tell her friend the pilot hadn't remembered her until she pushed him in the direction of the office to say hello. 'You're not really getting ideas about him, I hope. You wouldn't be that daft?'

Pearl giggled and squeezed Charlotte's arm. 'You're worse than my mum. Of course I realise his type but he's like a breath of fresh air around the place. Our loss is Brighton's gain.'

'So, you wouldn't mind playing along if we happen to bump into Robert?'

'Robert Costello?'

'Of course. I think he's got the wrong impression about me. If you and Philip look as if you only have eyes for one another, I'm sure it'll help convince Robert I look upon Philip as a friend.'

Pearl unlinked her arm from Charlie's and stopped walking. 'How long have you had your eye on Robert? You didn't say anything to me and we usually tell each other things.' She sounded puzzled and a little hurt.

Charlie took a deep breath. 'I know. I'm very sorry but it's all happened so quickly.'

Pearl nodded. 'I saw you talking to Robert the afternoon we went to watch Philip fly.'

'Let's go on walking,' said Charlie. 'Robert was a bit sarcastic that afternoon. I did tell you that.'

'You did. And I asked you why you thought he was ribbing you. You didn't give me a very convincing answer and you completely ignored my next question.'

'Did I?'

'Come off it, Charlie. If you like the fellow, why not admit it?'

They stopped as they neared the promenade and leaned on the railing to gaze at the ocean sparkling in the sunshine.

'I do like Robert but I didn't realise how much until he said he'd ring me. But he still hasn't and I'm convinced he thinks I've fallen for Philip.'

'Oh, Charlie, that's awful. I always thought Robert was a serious young man. A hard worker. Come to think of it, he's perfect for you.'

'I don't know about that — being perfect for me, I mean. But yes, he's a hard worker and I do like him very much. But he's got this bee in his bonnet about Philip and he couldn't be more wrong. I can't just march up to him and tell him he has to take me out so that's why I'm hoping Philip and you will do the trick.'

'The things I do for friendship! But if cuddling up to a handsome pilot will solve your problem, you can count on me. Have you had a chance to explain to Phil what he's in for?'

'When he came round to collect the tea tray,' Charlotte said, brown eyes gleaming, 'he told me it would be a pleasure to escort two such beautiful young ladies and he couldn't wait to get you all to himself on the ghost train!'

Pearl laughed out loud. 'Maybe he'll get a shock when I slap his face.'

'But you don't mind a bit of play-acting so Robert gets the message?'

'Guide's honour, though I certainly shan't fall in love with Philip. I . . .'

'You what? Go on Pearl. Now who is it who won't confess her feelings to her best friend?'

'Please don't make me tell you!'

'Do I know this young man of yours?'

'Yes, but shut up, Charlie please. Philip's just turned the corner and I need to start acting as if he's the only man in the world for me, don't I?' She fluttered her eyelashes. 'Is this the kind of thing you're looking for?'

★　★　★

Charlotte's stomach was acting as though a large bird, wearing heavy boots, was jumping up and down inside it. Across the way, she could see Robert, in charge of the big carousel. The gilded horses, dressed up to the nines with vivid colours and flowing manes, glided up and down, up and down, as the roundabout rotated. The fairground organ belted out a catchy tune while Rainbow, Prince, Ivanhoe and their fellow steeds transported the riders on their circular journey.

Charlotte watched Robert stare at the fiendish gaping mouth of the Ghost Train, towards which a car containing Pearl and Philip trundled purposefully.

He watched the pilot put a protective arm around Pearl's shoulders then he turned in Charlotte's direction, catching her eye. His face lit up and he mouthed something to her, something undecipherable but she understood he wanted her to wait. A feeling of relief, warm and comforting as hot chocolate spread throughout her though she knew her father was unlikely to approve of this young man as a potential boyfriend, let alone husband. What was happening to her? She and Robert hadn't even walked out together on a proper date and here she was, allowing her imagination to misbehave.

When the carousel lost impetus and slowed to a halt, Robert helped one or two younger riders dismount from their horses. Charlotte watched him, noting his gentleness and patience. He caught one small boy whose foot slipped and saved him from a nasty tumble. The child's mother thanked Robert then, his duties fulfilled, he ignored the usual method of returning to the ground and leapt from the platform, landing a few feet away from Charlotte.

'Hello,' he said. 'Does your father know you've escaped?'

'Ha hah, very funny. As it happens, I've had almost all of today off.'

Robert's knowing smile showed his awareness that no such thing existed in their lives.

'I had to go on an errand today and I saw you out shopping,' he said. 'What are you up to then, if I may make so bold? Maybe playing chaperone to the happy couple?' He gestured towards the Ghost Train, its forefront awash with pointing bony fingers, grinning skulls and dancing skeletons. The sound of the unfortunate patrons' screams echoed through the sound system together with blood-curdling cackles. 'How long has that romance been going on?'

'Philip leaves Peel Bay soon. I thought it would be a friendly gesture to make an evening of it, especially as I hadn't heard from you.' She held her breath, hoping he wouldn't snap at her.

'I see. And will your lover boy miss Pearl, I wonder — or will he miss you most of all?'

'He's not my lover boy!' She gestured towards the Ghost Train. 'He and Pearl are enjoying being together for a few hours, that's all. The flying circus moves to Brighton next week and as for the future, I imagine he'll do his duty,' she said. 'If there's really going to be a war, that is.'

'I think we all know there will be,' said Robert. 'I imagine the Air Force will snap him up. Fair play, he must know what he's about if he can keep that matchbox airborne.'

'And who's going to snap you up, Robert?' Her eyes challenged him.

They moved slowly away from the bright lights towards the fence beyond which lay the kiddies' boating lake. It was in darkness, miniature craft with nowhere to go, covered and clustered at one end.

She longed to tell him how she felt. How she knew she could tolerate all the inconveniences and hardships of fighting a war on the home front, as long as she knew he was coming home to her. She knew he must have dreams, even though of course he hadn't shared them with her. They both had their adult lives in front of them but Charlotte, although well aware that in his eyes, she was probably the garage proprietor's daughter with her nose in the air, longed to become his sweetheart.

Deep down, she feared his mock jealousy of Philip was just a smoke-screen. She feared Robert hesitated to ask her to go out with him because the Costellos were viewed by many in the town as not the right kind of people to socialise with. And a father who could afford to let his daughter drive his car and visit the fair now and then, dressed in her pretty clothes, wouldn't want her to end up marrying into the Costello clan.

At last he said, 'I shall go where I'm sent, of course.'

'Well, if it comes to it, I'd like to join the WAAFs,' she said. 'I think I'd enjoy that.'

Robert sighed. 'I think you might change your mind once reality set in. Have you given any thought to what might happen if your father decides to enlist?'

She ignored his first jibe but not the second. 'Dad's too old to go off and fight again!'

'He is for active service, yes, but an experienced motor engineer like him would be welcomed with open arms. And Don's the same age as me. You need to face up to all this, Charlotte.'

She bit her lip, hearing Robert say what her brother had already made plain. 'I could say the same to you.' Charlotte held her breath. This provocative statement might result in something she didn't want to hear but it was too late now.

'Charlotte, there's nothing left to

run. Takings this season are down on last year's and those were lousy. Costello's Funfair will be shutting down early this year and for more than just the winter. This war's seen to that. I don't know what my dad's going to do because he's not in the best of health. But your dad's fit enough to pass the medical, which means, if he decides to enlist, somebody's going to have to run that garage. Surely you can see that?'

She gasped as if she'd been douched with icy water. 'But he wouldn't trust me with it! It's a man's job.'

'I'm sorry, but it's high time you faced facts.'

She rounded on him. 'What's Don been saying? Why don't they ever discuss things with me? It's because I'm a girl, isn't it?'

The eerie wails from the Ghost Train, the rhythmic notes of the barrel organ and the stallholders' cries all faded away as Robert took Charlotte in his arms. If any would-be riders were clambering onto the horses, neither of

71

them noticed as boy and girl clung together. As if it was the most natural thing in the world, she tilted her chin and her lips met his. Even when their first tentative kiss ended, they still held on to each other as if neither could bear to let go of the other.

'I know I'm not good enough for you, Charlotte,' he whispered against her hair at last.

'I don't ever want to hear such a stupid remark again,' she said. 'It's just not true.'

Gently Robert distanced himself from her and took each of her hands in his. 'I got cold feet about asking you to come out with me, wondering what your father would say. Then when I saw you with Philip today, I thought . . . well, you can imagine what I thought.'

'Well, you thought wrong, didn't you? I talk to lots of men at the garage, young and old! You should know that. And between you and me, Pearl's got her head screwed on. She just wants a night out, having a bit of harmless fun and who can blame her?'

'Who indeed? So, how about next Wednesday, Charlie? I don't want to get you into trouble with your father but would you allow me to escort you to the pictures?'

Her heart flip-flopped as delight flooded her. 'I'd like that very much and I don't think for one minute, my dad would object.' She hesitated, ever practical. 'Are you sure you can have the night off?'

Robert's jaw tightened. 'I'm quite sure. From now on, we'll be opening weekends only. After that . . . ' He swallowed and turned away from Charlotte, folding his arms.

She stood, unsure whether to give him a hug, afraid to crowd him, knowing they both stood on the brink of uncertainty.

The mood was broken as Charlotte heard Philip call her name. She turned her head to see the pilot, hand in hand with a laughing Pearl, who he tugged along behind as he loped towards them.

She felt a surge of joy as Robert moved closer, putting his arm around her waist.

'Hey, you two,' said Philip. 'What are you doing lurking in the shadows — as if I couldn't guess.'

Charlotte answered quickly, not wanting Robert to make some sarcastic remark about not all men being the same as the pilot. 'We were talking business,' she said.

Philip nodded his head. 'We believe you, don't we sweetheart?'

'Of course,' Pearl said, snuggling up to him.

Philip took no notice. 'How are you two fixed this weekend? Pearl's been telling me about this Saturday tea dance she fancies going to. We could make up a foursome if you fancy the idea.'

Charlotte bit her lip, anticipating what she knew Robert would say. She rarely attended one of these events, usually finding herself too busy though Pearl had often nagged her to make time to go with her. Her friend was smiling now, looking expectant.

'I'm sorry,' said Robert. 'I really can't desert my father on a Saturday. There won't be many more opportunities to earn money before we close down for the season.' He squeezed Charlotte's waist a little harder, letting her know he wasn't minded to confess the sad truth underlying his remark.

'I'm sorry but I can't make it either,' she said quickly. 'Why don't you two go on your own?'

'That's a shame,' said Philip. 'But duty must come before pleasure. How about it then, Pearl?'

'I'd love to go,' said Pearl. She looked at Charlotte. 'Why don't you tell Don what we're planning? If you're working, he must be free?'

Charlotte nodded but pulled a face. 'He mightn't want to risk bumping into Kitty. It'd be awful if she turned up with another victim in tow.'

Philip turned to Pearl. 'Does this mean I'll have to compete for a dance with you?' He put on a hurt puppy-dog expression.

Pearl laughed. 'No, it means I need someone to talk to while you flit away to dance with every pretty girl in the room.'

'I shall do no such thing,' he said, 'because I shall be dancing with her anyway.'

Even Robert roared with laughter. Philip was incorrigible and Charlotte knew she'd miss the pilot when he left. He had the gift of being able to lighten the moment and goodness knows they'd all be looking for some of that in the coming weeks and months.

'I'll speak to Don,' she said. 'But don't be surprised if he says two's company and three's a crowd.'

Time Running Out

Charlotte was timing boiled eggs for breakfast as Don walked into the kitchen.

'I can't get used to you looking so smart,' he said. 'I keep wondering who it is in the kitchen when I see you from behind.'

'It's not that dramatic a change. Dad hasn't even noticed my new hairdo.'

Don began opening a can of tinned grapefruit to divide among the three bowls. 'Other things on his mind, sis. I must say your new look is a definite improvement. Mind you, the only way was up.'

He ducked as his sister aimed the tea towel at him and fielded it smartly. 'Was the hairdo meant to impress the fly boy? You seem to have got quite friendly with him recently, just as I was beginning to suspect you and Robert might have something going for you.'

Charlotte turned off the gas beneath the egg pan and put her hands on her hips. 'Friendly is the operative word,' she said firmly. 'If you want to know, Maggie in the greengrocers told me I needed to take more care of my appearance so I took the hint.' Deliberately she didn't comment on Don's reference to Robert.

Don placed the bowls of fruit on the table and took his seat.

'I happen to know Pearl and Philip are going to the tea dance at Randalls this afternoon. Pearl wondered if you fancied joining them.'

He raised his eyebrows. 'What, and play gooseberry? I don't like the sound of that.'

'It's not that kind of outing. Pearl suggested the idea to Philip then they asked me and Robert but we both said no because we were working and then Pearl asked me to ask you if you'd like to go along. Obviously you don't have to go as a couple.' She ended in a rush.

'Whoa!' Donald raised his hands in the air. 'Does your friend feel sorry for me?'

'Don't be daft. To tell the truth, I think she'd be glad of some company. Phil's a bit hard to handle sometimes — he's such a flirt. I think Pearl wants to dance and she knows Mum taught you well. I seem to have inherited Dad's sense of rhythm, which is nonexistent.'

'You're not playing matchmaker are you, Charlie? I hope not, because it won't do any good. I'm not looking for a girlfriend just at the moment.' He looked at the big round kitchen clock. 'I heard the doorbell earlier. Guess Dad had to go and help out some stranded motorist.'

'Sorry,' said Charlotte. 'Meant to say he'll come round for his breakfast once you've had yours. I seem to have a lot on my mind at the moment.'

'Am I right in thinking Robert Costello could be one of those things on your mind? These bread rolls are nice, by the way.'

She passed him his boiled eggs. 'I didn't want to talk about Robert, after your unfortunate experience with Kitty.'

Don sighed. 'The brush off didn't come as a complete surprise.'

'You had doubts, I know.' She sat down opposite him. 'Even so, the way she did it was rotten.'

'Like Dad said, worse things happen at sea. Now come on, tell me how the big love affair's going.' He looked up from his plate. 'Oh what fun it is to make my little sister blush.'

'What makes you think it's a love affair?' She spoke casually as she sliced off the top of her egg.

Don's smile was wistful. 'Oh, no particular reason, it's just that all the time I've known Robert, he's never ever fallen for a girl before.'

Charlotte's spoon clattered on to her plate. 'You can't be sure of that.'

Don scraped the last of his egg from the shell. 'I am sure, as it happens. Put that in your pipe and smoke it, little sister.'

Her breath seemed to lodge in her lungs as Charlotte took in what her brother said. How long had Robert felt this way? Would he kiss her again when they had the cinema date? Or would he be worried about rushing things? She pushed her daydreams away, anxious to sort out her brother's social life while she had him on his own.

'I wish you'd go along with Pearl and Philip,' she said. 'I know she's disappointed I can't join them. Having you there would make it more enjoyable for her. I know it would.'

Don poured himself another cup of tea. 'I mustn't be too long but knowing you, this idea of yours will turn up again at dinner time. I never bothered looking out my suit and shirt after you know who decided to give me the heave-ho. You haven't given me much notice, sis.'

She grinned at him. 'Nor any room for excuses, Don. I've given your suit a good brushing and ironed your best shirt, found a tie plus polished your black shoes. I would say, brother dear, you definitely owe me a bar of my favourite milk chocolate.'

★　★　★

That afternoon, Don was despatched to pick up Pearl and to drive her to Randalls, the popular ballroom built on the headland and approached by a winding road leading up from the old harbour.

Charlotte hoped her brother would enjoy his afternoon. He worked very hard, often taking things very seriously indeed. She knew he was concerned about the effect a war would have on them. Everyone faced the same situation but their own little family was already missing a very vital and much-loved member. It was good to see Don go off looking so handsome. He might even meet some nice girl and forget all about cruel Kitty as

Charlotte privately dubbed his former girlfriend.

'I'm sorry you couldn't go dancing too, love.' Mr Moore looked round as she wandered into the workshop between customers at the pumps.

'It's all right Dad. I thought Don could do with a bit of a treat. I was much more anxious for him to go than for me. Especially as ... um, I mean ...' She was left floundering, hands in the pockets of her hard-wearing overalls.

Mr Moore's head was hidden once again by the bonnet of the car he was fixing. It hadn't stopped him from hearing what his daughter said, though.

'I suppose you mean the Costello boy's working this afternoon so he can't go either.'

Charlie looked down at her dirty fingernails and wrinkled her nose. 'Robert's asked me to go out with him, Dad. I'm sorry I haven't mentioned it to you but he only asked me last night, down at the fair.'

'You need a social life, love. As long as he doesn't try any Wall of Death stunts on that bike of his, I don't have a problem with you walking out with him.'

'Walking out — how old-fashioned that sounds, Dad! But thanks for not saying I shouldn't go.'

'I am old-fashioned, love. I like the old-fashioned values and that's why I want to see them preserved. But don't let me get on my hobbyhorse. What I want to say to you is that the Costello family are grafters. They've been hit hard by the slump and now the war's increasing the damage. Very soon, I think we'll hear a formal announcement from Mr Chamberlain. Decisions will need to be made.'

He paused then smiled at his daughter. 'In the meantime, you young folk should try to enjoy yourselves while the going's good. I don't mean you should ever forget you're a decent young lady, Charlotte. Lads will be lads and I'm sure I don't have to spell it out to you. Now, pass me that screwdriver will you?'

She obeyed, her cheeks hot with embarrassment. Phew. She hadn't expected her father to show quite so much understanding about Robert but she was delighted to hear he respected him. So much for Robert's uncertainty! She had both her dad and her brother on her side and that gave her a wonderful feeling. In fact, it was almost like being in love.

A car cruised on to the forecourt and hearing it, Charlotte hurried outside, ready to approach the driver's window. 'Hello, Sir,' she said. 'Is it your usual two gallons of Super, today?'

★ ★ ★

Don came home later, in good spirits. In fact it was much, much later than Charlotte had anticipated. She saw him drive the family car past the garage, ready to park round at the back and hurried through, to open up the double doors for him.

'Did you enjoy it? How many dances did you have? What was the tea like? Did you have a cocktail?'

'Hey, let me get out of the car first,' said Don. 'I'll shut the doors. You'd better go back outside in case a customer arrives without you noticing.'

'All right, but don't you dare disappear in the house. I want a full report. Immediately.'

Sunshine still bathed the forecourt so Charlie went back and perched on one of the stools that, in fine weather, they put out either side of the entrance to the office. Her father was in the house, having finished his tricky repair task and gone to get cleaned up.

Don joined his sister. 'The band played *In the Mood* and your friend and I had a circle round us when we were jitterbugging.'

'Oh, I wish I'd seen you,' Charlie wailed. 'I'm so glad you had fun though. I bet Pearl enjoyed being the centre of attention.'

'She seemed happy enough. I think I surprised Philip too. He complimented me on my technique. We got on quite well, especially after we found we both liked cricket. After all, he can't be too bad a bloke if Dad enjoys his company.'

Charlie raised her eyes heavenwards. 'First engines, now sport. Poor Pearl — I hope you didn't ignore her too much.'

'Not at all. Philip seemed to take a fancy to a girl he danced with during the Paul Jones so he brought her back to the table to introduce her. Nice girl. She was there with her brother, apparently.'

'Is she local?'

'She lives in Coynesbury. There weren't that many familiar faces there. Maybe the tea dances are seen as being a bit posh for most of the people we know. A fellow can't turn up unless he's wearing a suit.'

'So, you and Pearl hit it off on the dance floor?'

'Um, yes. I suppose you could say that.'

Charlie looked at her watch. 'It's time to close up. Come to think of it, what took you so long to get home?'

'Um, well, you see, it being a nice evening, I suggested a little walk along the promenade. We didn't go near the fair.' He shot his sister a sly glance. 'So we didn't see Robert.'

'The three of you went for a walk?'

'Well, Pearl and I walked. The last I saw of Philip, he was still in the bar with that girl he met and her brother.'

Charlie decided to say no more. Knowing Don had enjoyed a few hours' relaxation and fun meant a lot to her. Further interrogation could wait until another time.

'Come on Fred Astaire,' she said. 'Help me check everything's locked away then we'll go and have a bit of supper with Dad.'

* * *

Philip, having promised to write to at least ten hopeful young ladies, flew his aeroplane off into the blue yonder — more accurately, in the direction of Brighton, his mechanic packing up after him and driving the van sign-written with Flying Circus insignia.

A hint of autumn sharpened the early mornings even though it wasn't yet September. A hint of menace made Charlotte shiver when she heard a news bulletin or sat down to read the daily paper if she found time. Words like mobilisation, neutrality and ultimatum were sprinkled like currants over the heavy dough of radio broadcasts and newspaper reports. Charlotte hadn't even heard of the Registrar General but she knew he was the person who announced the distribution of identity cards and numbers for everyone in the event of a full-blown war. Speculation as to what would happen next coloured conversations with customers and with the shopkeepers and café owners when Charlotte managed to meet Pearl for a cup of tea during a break from their duties.

In these days of uncertainty, there was one thing about which Charlotte was absolutely certain. The day of her cinema outing with Robert, she met Pearl for a cup of coffee, each stealing a few minutes from shopping time.

'You know I'm seeing Robert this evening?' Charlotte passed the sugar bowl across the table. 'We'll have to get used to rationing soon. I'm trying to cut down on sugar — a tiny bit less each time. Hope it works.'

'Ugh,' said Pearl. 'I'll happily have your share.'

'It's all right for you — you're built like a hairpin. I can do with a bit of fine tuning.'

Pearl giggled. 'You sound just like a mechanic. Maybe I should learn a bit more about spark plugs and radiators.'

Charlotte leaned forward. 'So you can converse knowledgeably with my brother, by any chance?'

'Tut tut,' said Pearl. 'Now, did I say

that? Maybe I think a bit more know-how would help me when I'm typing up the customers' bills. Your dad's writing's a bit like a doctor's scribble, seems to me.'

'You have my sympathies. I'd much rather cook for the two of them than decipher their handwriting.'

'Never mind me. Where's Robert taking you tonight?'

'We're going to the Tivoli.'

'Is he picking you up on his bike?'

'He's coming in to say hello to Dad then we're walking down. It's only ten minutes after all.'

Pearl sat back in her chair. 'Sounds like he's getting his feet under the table. Has he kissed you yet?'

Charlie looked around, her expression alarmed. 'Shush! Would you like me to fetch a megaphone so you can be sure you're broadcasting my business to all and sundry?'

Both girls giggled.

'I'm just so pleased for you, Charlie,' said Pearl. 'You two make a lovely couple — Robert so dark and you the golden girl. Can I be your bridesmaid when the big day comes?'

Charlie knew her cheeks were turning to beetroot. It was far too soon to think along those lines, yet as soon as the suggestion fell from Pearl's lips, she knew that was where she hoped her destiny would lie. As to whether Robert felt the same, that was another matter. Their romance was too new, too fragile, for her to be totally confident. She felt sure of her own feelings but some might say she and Robert were rushing into romance as a respite from the dark days lying ahead.

'All right, you don't have to answer that,' said Pearl, a little smile upturning the corners of her mouth. 'But it can't hurt to dream, surely?'

*   *   *

Charlotte glanced up at the clock. She and Robert needed to start walking to the cinema if they were to be sure of seeing the start of the show. Her father was talking about his recollections of the funfair, at a time before the Costello family took it over. Robert was either fascinated or making a very good attempt at seeming so.

She waited for a pause in the conversation. 'Dad, I'm sorry to interrupt but time's going on.'

Mr Moore pushed back his chair. 'I need to get round to the garage anyway. Sorry, Robert, I didn't mean to monopolise you.'

Robert rose too and held out his hand. 'Thank you for the tea and scones, Sir. I've enjoyed talking to you.'

'Charlotte's a dab hand at scone making. Drop in any time you like. And you won't forget to mention my idea to your father?'

'I certainly shan't. I understand your feelings and I know he will too. It's as well to be prepared, I think.'

Charlotte reached for her cardigan.

Her father cleared his throat. 'From now on, you should call me Raymond.

Then I won't feel quite so ancient.' He winked at Charlotte. 'Enjoy the show.'

The three of them left the kitchen together, Mr Moore locking the door behind them. Charlotte and Robert set off towards the high street. She felt a bubble of joy as he reached for her hand and clasped it firmly in his. They were still in sight of the garage and Robert's seemingly small gesture meant a great deal to her. She couldn't really explain how she felt but it was as if they truly were courting now, not merely stepping out to the cinema.

'Did you see that brother of mine on your way, earlier?'

'I did. We had time for a quick chat,' said Robert. 'He told me to take good care of you.' He squeezed her hand.

'My word. I'm surprised you didn't get teased.'

'Oh, there was a bit of that as well. I can take it.'

'Hmm. Next time, I shall have to get out some photographs of Donald as a baby.' She gasped. 'Oh dear, I'm sorry,

Robert. That sounds very forward of me. You mightn't want to repeat the experience.'

Gently he released her hand and put his arm round her waist. She held her breath and in her turn moved her own arm, adjusting her step, so they walked smoothly together. Neither said a word. Neither needed to.

When they reached the cinema Robert purchased two seats in the dress circle. Charlie, very aware of his family's precarious position, had to bite her lip, wanting to offer to pay her share but worried she might embarrass him.

He smiled at her as he turned from the ticket office. 'Would you like some bonbons, Charlie?'

'Oh, no thanks,' she said. 'I'm trying to curb my sweet tooth.'

'You're not on one of these new-fangled diets, surely?'

They walked towards the staircase.

'I could do with losing a few pounds,' she said, unwilling to bring up the subject of war.

'What rubbish. You're fine as you are.'

They took their seats just in time for the newsreel. The usherette, leading the way with her torch beam, showed them to the back row, much to Charlotte's embarrassment. They whispered apologies, squeezing past two pairs of knees before they could sit down.

As Charlotte might have anticipated, the newsreel contained quite enough on the subject of Germany and those countries determined to stand up to her. Seeing the images of troops and warships on the big screen highlighted the situation in no uncertain way. A quick glance at Robert's profile showed his clenched jaw. As if sensing her feelings, he reached for her hand and she let it lie, lightly clasped in his, on the arm of the seat between them. It was only when the familiar roaring lion emblem disappeared from the screen and the main film began that Robert placed his arm round her shoulders. She snuggled closer to him as if it was the most natural thing in the world.

I wish Mum could know how happy I am with this young man, thought Charlotte. Once more, she prayed for sanity in the world although she feared this was too much to hope. Meanwhile, she intended to enjoy Robert's company as much as possible.

★　★　★

Charlotte and Robert walked back together, hand in hand through the darkened streets, to her house.

'I really enjoyed that,' she said. 'Even though I found it a bit of a tear-jerker.'

'It's possible,' said Robert, 'the British government are well-pleased to have that film on general release at a time when lots of people are considering their positions.'

'How do you mean?'

'Mr Chips has to surmount lots of obstacles in order to prove his worth. When the First World War breaks out, he puts aside his retirement and takes up teaching again because so many younger teachers have to join up. The message is, experience tells.'

Charlotte bit her lip as she realised what Robert was getting at. Her father might well be contemplating this very situation, though of course he was a long way from retirement. Changes were definitely on the cards and lots of people would be taking up new roles not just in their own locality but much further afield.

They walked in silence, Charlotte wondering what the plan was that her dad had mentioned to Robert before they all left the kitchen. Suddenly Robert stopped walking and took both her hands in his.

'Whatever happens, Charlotte, I want you to know you mean the world to me. I never imagined feeling like this but I do and I just want you to know it, that's all. I'm not one for fancy talk but when the day comes for me to go away, I'd like to leave, knowing you're my girl. Knowing we'll write to each other, with the understanding that one day, God willing, I can ask you to marry me.'

Charlotte's heart bump bumped in her chest and her mouth dried. 'We haven't spent much time in each other's company,' she said, 'but I feel the same, Robert. We have no idea how everything will work out but somehow I feel it will.'

'My lovely girl,' he whispered, taking her in his arms right under the streetlamp. 'I hope your dad's not peeping through the curtains because I really do have to kiss you.'

After their brief but sweet kiss, he opened the gate for her and watched her take out her door key. 'Come and see me at the fair as soon as you can? I don't want to keep you out late.'

'I'll come the first afternoon I can,' she said. 'Goodnight, Robert.'

She heard him drive away as she locked and bolted the door behind her and walked through to the kitchen.

Her father looked up from his newspaper. 'There's a drop of cocoa left in the saucepan if you want to warm it up. Did you enjoy your film?'

She moved to the stove. 'Very much but it was thought-provoking. Speaking of which, Dad, don't you think it's time you came clean with me about your intentions once war's declared?'

Mr Moore put down his paper and twisted round in his chair as Charlotte lit the gas. 'It's not done just to annoy you, love — not broaching the subject, I mean. I suppose I've been hoping for a miracle but quite honestly, I'm just prolonging the agony.'

She stirred the chocolate mixture in the pan. 'Where's Don?'

'He went out to play football, came home and had a bath then decided on an early night.'

'I bolted the door so that's OK then.' She watched steam rise from the pan and switched off the gas.

Her father waited while she carried her drink to the table. 'You deserve to hear the truth from my own lips. Fact is, love, I'm determined to offer help

100

in some form or other when the time comes.' He held up his hand. 'No, please hear me out. If my old regiment will have me, I'll probably be deployed to help train young recruits as mechanics. That's something I know I can do and at least I'll feel I'm needed.'

'But you're needed here, Dad. The business needs you. I need you!' She lifted the mug to her mouth, her hand trembling. She took a gulp of cocoa and thumped her drink down on the table again. 'How the heck could I run the business all on my own? Just tell me that, would you?'

'Yes, I will tell you, my girl. First of all, you're more than capable of doing the job. If I didn't have faith in you, I'd not be volunteering. I'd sit tight here and swallow my pride. After all, I want to have something to hand down to you and Don. But of course you can't do the job all on your own. You must take me for a right chump!' He waited for her to smile back at him.

'I've spoken to your young man's dad.'

Charlotte's mouth opened in shock.

'George Costello, as you probably know, has decided to cease trading — not just over the winter months but for the foreseeable future. He's a bit creaky in the joints but more than capable of serving petrol and oil. He's got a good business head on his shoulders and his wife's used to bookkeeping so you wouldn't have to worry about that side of things, love, after Pearl leaves.'

'Phew, that's a relief.' Charlie's smile was shaky but she was beginning to make sense of all the mutterings and half-truths she'd been wondering about.

'There's no question of Don not joining up so we'll need to recruit an apprentice. I've asked around and there's a lad who'll do nicely, I reckon. It's young Jack — you know him already and he's keen to work. You'll have a good team around you and even though George Costello's past it as regards lying under motor vehicles to mend them, he can teach Jack the basics. I've asked the boy to turn up tomorrow so I can give him a bit of a talking to. No time like the present.'

Charlotte heaved a sigh. 'You're not even waiting for the announcement are you? You're that sure?'

'I'm sure all right, love. It's not a case of 'if' but a case of 'when'.'

'Why did you take your time about talking to me? Did you think I'd run away or something?' Charlotte tried not to sound hurt.

Her dad's smile was affectionate. 'You're a young woman with a young woman's hopes and dreams,' he said. 'I wanted you at least to have a short time when you could enjoy your new romance. The timing's terrible for you and Robert but with luck, we'll all come out of it at the end. Just you keep thinking that, Charlotte.'

'Dad,' she whispered. 'Mum would be proud of you, you know.'

Her father swallowed hard. 'And of you, love, that's for sure. Now give your old dad a hug then I reckon we'll call it a night, what say you?'

Charlotte put her arms round her father. 'One more thing, Dad — what did you mean about Pearl? Is she giving up doing our books? She's not said anything to me.'

'She's probably waiting for the announcement but don't you think, when the whole thing swings into operation, Pearl will decide to volunteer? They won't call her up yet but from little things she's said lately, I wouldn't be surprised to see her apply for a job in a munitions factory, even join one of the women's forces.'

At that moment, Charlotte felt a surge of panic. She'd been thinking of her menfolk and totally forgetting the women were in this too. 'I suppose I'm being selfish but I'd assumed she'd stay and help me.'

'When you reach twenty, you'll need to be registered as carrying out a necessary role in my absence. I don't know the whys and wherefores yet but that'll come. Pearl's very useful to us but an older man or woman not eligible for call-up could easily replace her. She knows that.' His voice softened. 'It's not about friendship you know, it's about saving our country. Now, we'd better get our heads down, love. It'll all be sorted out as time goes by, don't you fret.'

* * *

Next morning, with her father out helping the town's mayor to get his car back on the road, Charlie was able to have a quick chat with her brother.

'Dad's finally told me what he's been mulling over,' she said as she dished up bowls of porridge. It was a chilly morning and having risen early, she'd put a pan on to simmer.

Don reached for the can of golden syrup. 'About time,' he said. 'Mind you, I didn't know all of it. He mentioned taking on a youngster to me but he only told me about Mr and Mrs Costello last night. I don't think Robert even knew. It's a good idea, though.'

'Yes,' said Charlotte cautiously. 'I haven't met them yet, remember.'

Don licked his spoon. 'I've only met them a couple of times. You must have seen Robert's dad at the fair, surely? And Mrs Costello often sells the Wall of Death tickets of an evening.'

'There was an older lady with dark brown hair coiled up in a bun, the night I went over there and Robert took me to the Velvet.' She looked expectantly at Don.

'That sounds like you saw Mrs C.'

'She never said anything to me about being Robert's mum but she was very cheerful and friendly.'

'The show must go on, I suppose, like here, in a way. We might feel a bit off-colour, might not feel like talking about the weather or whatever, but the customer expects our attention.'

'The customer's always right, as Dad

says.' She suddenly remembered her trip to the hairdresser. 'Eleanor said the same to me when she was doing my hair, come to think of it.'

Don nodded. 'Regular customers are worth hanging on to. First timers might become regulars, unless they live miles away. It's not a bad thing to remember.'

'Don't fret, Don. I'll even apply that rule to Mr Ghastly Greener.'

He shook his head and tilted his bowl to scrape up the last spoonful of porridge. 'Now that, dear sister, is asking a lot. But I have faith in you.'

Charlotte chuckled. 'Praise indeed. Now get off with you and open up. It's washing day but I'll bring some tea round as soon as I can.'

'Good girl. Um, is, um, Pearl in today by any chance?'

Charlie couldn't hide her grin. 'She's due in this afternoon, as it happens.'

'Right, then.'

'Well, don't leave me in suspense! Are you going to ask her out?'

He tapped the side of his nose.

'That'd be telling.'

'See if I care. I'll get it out of Pearl anyway, that's for sure.'

'Women!' But Don was smiling.

Charlotte liked things tidy. Also, a happy brother was far easier to deal with than one still stewing over a failed friendship. With a bit of luck, Pearl and Don might also be able to enjoy some fun and companionship during these last fragile days of peace.

★ ★ ★

A couple of evenings later, Charlotte took the bus from the Corner Garage stop to the promenade. She'd asked to borrow the car, hoping to save some time but Mr Moore put his foot down and told them both he needed it himself that evening.

'Wonder what he's up to?' Don said to Charlotte when she called into the office on her way out that evening.

'I've no idea,' she said. 'He can't be going to visit Robert's parents because

I'm sure he'd have offered me a lift.'

Robert peered through the window. 'Your bus is on the way. I expect Robert will bring you home.'

Charlotte picked up her bag from the counter. 'You still haven't said anything about you and Pearl.'

'I'm biding my time,' he said. 'I have my reasons.'

Both Dad and Don were being most mysterious, thought Charlotte as she hurried to the bus stop. The news about Germany invading Poland had probably interfered with her brother's plans to court Pearl, if that had been his intention. She didn't like secrets but now she had other things on her mind, things that, like this last chilling announcement, needed to be dealt with.

She climbed up on to the top deck and when the conductor appeared, requested a single ticket. Even if Robert couldn't bring her home later, she didn't mind walking back. Her father's efforts to clean up early and even shave for the second time that day still puzzled her. But as soon as the bus lumbered along the road to the old harbour on its approach to the promenade, she was down the stairs and standing on the platform, clutching the handrail ready to jump off and go to find Robert.

She headed for the entrance around the side, anticipating the main entrance would be closed. To her relief, the small door was unlocked and she slipped inside and round the Wall of Death arena towards the big carousel, which seemed to hold an aura of sadness, standing silent and stripped of its bright lights.

Over at the ghost train she spotted Robert. His back was towards her as he tapped at one of the boards with a hammer, so she tiptoed as quietly as she could until she was almost within touching distance.

'Wooh . . . woohoo,' she wailed. 'I've come to get you . . .'

Robert swung round and rose swiftly

to his feet. He placed his hammer on top of the little flight of steps leading to the train platform. 'You make a delightful ghost,' he said, hugging her to him. 'I like the sound effects.'

'I was going to ring and see if it was all right to come over but Don was on the phone then it went out of my head.'

'You forgot all about me? Huh!' He pulled a woebegone face.

She giggled. 'Hardly! I meant I forgot to make the phone call. I do think about you quite a lot, you know.'

He still held on to her hands. 'That's good, because I think about you too, Miss Moore.'

'As long as they're good thoughts,' she said.

'Always. Now, my parents are in the house and they'd like us to go and have a cup of tea with them. Is that all right?'

'Well, yes,' she said. 'I suppose this is all to do with what Dad told me the other day — his plans for the future.'

Robert nodded. 'It's a weight off my mind to think of my father having employment,' he said. 'My mother's come up with an idea too. She's thinking of offering bed and breakfast though she probably won't have much trade over the winter. I think it's a good idea. The house has four bedrooms and,' he hesitated, 'with me gone, they'll only have need of one.'

Charlie hid her face in his shoulder. 'I don't want to think about you going away.'

'I know, sweetheart,' he said. 'But I'm about to turn twenty and we have to face up to the situation. Whatever happens, it's a relief for me to know you'll have people around that you can trust and who will care about you.'

She nodded. 'Dad's thought things through and I'll do my best to cope but thank goodness your mum can keep books. That's such a relief.'

'Good. Now, unless you want a tour of the ghost train, I think I'm done for the evening. I just need to put away these steps and my box of tools.'

'Could I have a peep inside? The

ghost train ride, I mean.'

He laughed. 'Come on then. I'll shine my torch for you then you can see grisly ghouls to your heart's content.'

Charlotte followed him on to the platform and stepped gingerly down to the lower level where twin metal rails snaked beneath double doors painted with gnarled tree branches. These resembled skeletal arms ending in claws and she was quite relieved when Robert reached for her hand then pushed open the doors.

They walked into blackness. Robert shone his torch upwards and Charlotte saw giant spiders suspended from thick cobwebs and little black bats whose eyes glowed like hot coals in the beam of light. An owl perched on a tree branch, its huge eyes gleaming as Robert swivelled the torch in its direction.

'Goodness,' she said. 'It's so realistic.'

'Only when it's in darkness,' he said. 'If I put the overhead lights on, which we do of course when we need to fix something, you'd think it looked very tame compared to now. It's quite a complicated set-up, what with the sound effects as well. You should come along next weekend and sample the real thing, Charlie. Feel the cobwebs brush your cheek as you glide by.'

'Ugh! We'll have to see about that,' she said. 'Thanks for showing me though. When you shone the torch around, I could see how cleverly it's designed, considering it's not a very big space.'

'Tricks of the trade,' he said as they turned to make their way out.

Despite knowing nothing macabre lurked within the ghost train ride's innards, Charlie felt relieved when the staff door opened easily into the soft evening light.

'I should have brought your mother some flowers,' she said while Robert put away his kit and secured everything.

'Don't worry,' he said. 'She'll be pleased if you just bring yourself.'

They walked through the deserted

fairground and through the unmarked entrance Charlie had used on her way in. Robert slid the bolt across and clicked the padlock into place.

As they walked up the road leading to his home, he squeezed her hand. 'Only one more weekend's trading,' he said.

'What do you normally do during the off-season?' She realised this was something she'd never thought about before.

'There's always maintenance come September. We try and do as much as we can then take a short holiday somewhere, maybe with family back in Ireland. Having an aunt living in London's quite handy because she loves to come on holiday to the seaside, which means we have an open invitation to go and stay with her.'

They crossed the road. 'This year, of course, is a different matter.' He paused, as if finding the words difficult to say. 'My father won't be opening the fair again next year, that's for sure.'

'No, but he'll have plenty to do, won't he?'

Robert stopped. 'Thanks to your father, he will. It'll take some of the worry away and that can't be a bad thing.'

Charlotte almost blurted out there'd be other, potentially much more dangerous things to face but thought better of it. 'Do I look tidy?' she asked.

'You look lovely,' he said. 'Come on. You can meet them properly now. They're just ordinary people,' he added. 'Please don't be nervous.'

The evening had turned chillier and she shivered as he unlocked his front door. 'After braving things that go bump in the night, I should be perfectly able to face your folks,' she said.

'They're not the problem,' said Robert. 'I forgot to tell you about our big, bad hound. He's called Smuggler.'

'Oh dear, I'm not really used to dogs,' said Charlotte, wondering whether Smuggler would detect her feelings and take an instant dislike to

116

her. 'Um, how big exactly is he?'

A door at the end of the hallway opened and she whirled round to see the smiling face of the lady she remembered from the Wall of Death pay box. Along the carpet scampered a butterscotch coloured bundle of fur, resembling not so much a big, bad canine as a floppy-eared puppy. Charlotte dropped to her knees and opened out her arms so Smuggler could snuggle on her lap, while Robert's mother frowned at her son.

'Don't keep the poor young lady in the hallway,' she said. 'Bring her in for a warm by the range. You don't mind dogs, Charlotte? Say the word and I'll put Smuggler in the lean-to with his toys.'

Charlotte put the little dog gently down on the hall carpet and he scampered back towards the kitchen. She walked towards Mrs Costello, hand extended. 'Hello. I think Smuggler's lovely so please don't shut him away on my account.'

Robert's mother beamed at her and grasped her hand. 'Come and sit down, love. I'm looking forward to hearing all about you. Let's just get to know one another this evening, shall we?'

★ ★ ★

Next morning, Charlotte's father was eager to know how she'd got on.

'I really like Mrs Costello,' she told him, adding a fried egg to the tinned tomatoes on the big blue Delft china plate.

'Oh dear,' he said, reaching for the bread. 'I hope that doesn't mean George gets the thumbs down.'

'Gosh, no,' she said. 'Robert's dad is quieter, that's all. Takes a while to get to know you, I'd say.'

'I'd say, takes a while to get a word in with two ladies in the room,' said Don, pulling out his chair.

'Cheeky . . . you do want breakfast this morning, I suppose?'

Don bowed his head. 'Yes, please,

sister dear. So, did you enjoy your evening? Hope the news didn't put a damper on the occasion.'

'We tried to avoid unpleasant things — found lots to talk about, some sad but some very jolly.' She put Don's plate in front of him and brought her own to the table. 'Ah, thanks for pouring my tea, Dad. Did you have a nice evening?'

Her father blinked rapidly. 'Me? Oh, yes, I did, thank you. Just a bit of business I needed to discuss with someone.'

They ate in silence, Charlotte wondering who'd be first to broach the subject of the Prime Minister's speech. He'd have no alternative but to address the waiting nation soon.

Her father seemed to read her thoughts. 'Was that the letterbox I heard?'

'I'll go,' said Don. 'I expect you'd like a squint at the paper before we open up.'

Mr Moore and Charlotte continued

their meal in silence. Donald was back in a moment, the daily newspaper in his hand. He placed it beside his father's plate.

Charlotte and her brother exchanged glances as their father's gaze went straight to the headline.

'Not long to wait now,' he said.

★ ★ ★

On Sunday morning Mr Moore entered the kitchen through the side door and headed for the Bakelite radio on the shelf. He twiddled the knobs and settled himself at the table. A glance up at the clock showed him it was almost ten past eleven.

The door opened again. 'You've beaten me to it, Dad. Do you want me to go and relieve Don so he can hear what the Prime Minister has to say?'

'He's all right, Charlotte. I think he wants to carry on as normal as long as he possibly can.'

Charlotte nodded and put the laundry basket in a corner. 'The ironing still needs doing and the customers still need attending to.' She pulled out a chair.

The two sat in silence waiting for the announcement they dreaded but knew was inevitable. Mr Chamberlain didn't waste words when he told the nation their country was at war with Germany. Those words would stay locked in the memories of Charlotte's family, and those of countless others, for the rest of their lives.

Life Goes On

'There's something that's been worrying me, Charlotte, and at last I've come up with a solution.'

'Only one thing, Dad? If that's all then you're not doing too badly.'

'You know I'm relieved to have you managing the business, especially with Mr and Mrs Costello around?'

Charlotte nodded. 'We'll make sure things go well. It's going to be strange but we'll all do our best. It's a case of having to.'

'I'm afraid so. My problem has been the thought of you living here on your own, with Don and me both away.'

'I'll manage. It'll seem funny, cooking for one though.'

'How would you feel if your godmother moved in for a while?' His eyes focused on Charlotte's face.

'Auntie Eleanor move in here with

me? Whatever brought on that crazy idea?'

He spread his hands. 'At least give it some thought before you turn it down. I'd feel much happier, knowing you had company of a night.'

'What about her own business? Is she giving it up?'

'She's hoping ladies will still want their hair looking smart, even with Hitler trying to spoil the party. She'd go to the salon every morning but come here at close of business.'

Charlotte frowned. 'I'd sooner not have someone else to look after, Dad. Even having one more mouth to feed will take up precious time. Surely you haven't forgotten I'll have to do all the things you and Don usually do.'

'Eleanor realises that, love. I explained it all to her. She reckons she can make sure you have breakfast before you open up then she'll wash up, tidy round and go off to the salon. If she closes at five she'll have time to make a meal for both of you. George will do the last shift and shut up shop — once you're satisfied he knows the ropes, of course.'

Charlotte couldn't help feel a twinge of pride, thinking of herself as boss. 'But won't Eleanor miss having her own place with all her things around her?'

'She'll take her lunch break there as usual. She can nip out to do a bit of shopping for the two of you when necessary. And she's sorely missed having her own garden so she'll be able to dig out a few potatoes and use up whatever's going before winter sets in.'

'I was worried about the garden.' Charlotte gazed through the window. 'I suppose it could work. I've known her a good few years.' She chuckled. 'At least she won't let me forget to get my hair cut.'

Mr Moore sighed. 'It's not going to be easy for any of us but I rather like the idea of two people who mean a lot to me, being under one roof.'

Charlotte sat back and gaped at him. So he was fond of Eleanor? How fond

124

exactly did he mean? Had he been to visit her the evening she'd gone to see Robert and his parents? But her dad was pulling on the foreman's coat he'd worn for his garage work since Don finished his apprenticeship and took over as chief mechanic. Questions about her father's feelings for the woman who'd been a friend of both her parents since their schooldays could and must wait for another time.

* * *

Robert was to enlist in the Army. Many young men, because they'd already reached the age of twenty, had been called up for training. With his driving skills, including his knowledge of motorbikes, he thought he'd be ear-marked as a despatch rider. After his initial training he could be sent who knew where.

Charlotte knew it pleased her father when Don wanted to follow in his footsteps by applying to join the Army.

Her brother, whose birthday she now realised was only days after Robert's, wanted to make full use of his engineering skills. Occasionally she thought of Philip the Pilot who, a little older than Robert and Don, would be well on with his training by now.

Pearl, as forecast by Mr Moore, felt strongly about helping in any way she could.

'It's different for you, Charlie,' she said as they walked down the high street a couple of days after the Prime Minister's speech. 'You've already got an important job lined up. You know I was looking for some extra hours? Fate's about to hand them to me.'

'Dad thought you might go into Munitions.'

'I have something else in mind.' She stopped and looked at her friend. 'I'm going for an interview at the air base next week.'

Charlotte raised her eyebrows. 'You're joining up?'

'I hope to, later on. For now, I'm

after a job in the NAAFI. I like the idea of working somewhere different from a factory though I'll do it if it turns out that way. Mum's not too well at the moment so it'd be good if I could stay close to home.'

'But you won't be able to live at home, even if you get a posting to RAF Kimberley. Don't they have dormitories for the NAAFI staff?'

'Yes but I can cycle back when I get time off. Everything's changing, Charlie, even if not quite so much for you.'

'What? My life's about to change with a vengeance! Both Dad and Don are leaving home. I'd join up too, if I had any choice so please don't forget that.'

Pearl hugged Charlotte's arm. 'If the Corner Garage didn't exist, I know you'd go wherever you were called. I'm not as outgoing as you but I want to help instead of sitting quietly, working on sending bills and paying suppliers. I want to learn my way round people and catering seems to me a good way of doing so.'

'You seemed to get on very well with Philip when he was around.'

'Playing a part is different. Oh, I can't explain it very well but I think lots of us are going to be playing a part, for better or worse. I want to start off in a very minor way and see what happens.'

'Well, I think you're very brave.'

They walked on in silence for a while then Charlotte turned to Pearl. 'You will keep in touch?'

'Of course I will, you silly sausage. You're my best friend, aren't you?'

'You bet. And how about Don? Will you write to him, wherever he's posted? Or shouldn't I be so inquisitive?'

'If he wants me to, I'll write. He hasn't talked about it though.'

Charlotte shook her head. 'You two amaze me. Unless I've got it totally wrong, you're sweet on one another but you don't seem to be able to do much about it.'

'It's wartime. You can't blame people

for holding back rather than become involved, when none of us knows what's going to happen.'

Charlotte knew her friend wanted to seem worldly-wise but she suspected Pearl would like nothing more than to keep in touch with Don. She had a very wistful look in her eyes. Maybe a word with that brother of hers would do the trick.

'Pesky war,' she said. 'It's ruining everything. Everyone's going away and . . . and . . . '

Pearl clutched her friend's arm again. 'Don't finish that sentence,' she said. 'Concentrate on keeping things going and at least you'll be too busy to worry then.'

'I forgot to tell you,' said Charlotte. 'My godmother's moving in with me for a while, to see how we get on. Dad doesn't like the thought of me living in the house all alone.'

'My goodness,' said Pearl, stopping to look in a draper's window. She shot Charlotte a knowing look. 'Things are developing then?'

'Developing? Whatever do you mean?' She watched her friend's gaze slide away from hers.

'I didn't mean anything in particular,' said Pearl. 'Except your father's obviously thought of everything he can to help you. I'd expect nothing less.'

'I suppose not,' said Charlotte. 'I hope Eleanor and I won't rub one another up the wrong way though.'

'No time for that,' said Pearl. 'Not when there's work to be done.'

'You sound very self-assured. With all those new experiences heading your way, you'll probably think of me as a country bumpkin when you come home on leave.'

'You began to grow up after your mum died, Charlie. You may not have realised it, but the rest of us have. She'd be so, so proud of you.'

'That's funny. I said the same thing to my father recently. About Mum being proud of him, I mean.'

'She'd want you both to be happy,'

said Pearl. 'Now, I must get home and iron my grey costume ready for my interview.'

* * *

That evening, Eleanor was due to come round to have a look at the room Charlotte had prepared. The garage closed at six pm these evenings so Don and their father would be able to join the reception committee.

'It's only polite,' said Charlotte when Don suggested he might slip out for a couple of hours. 'At least stay to say hello. Eleanor will understand you want to make the most of your spare time, and see your friends.'

'I want to call on two people as it happens. For months it's been as if things were happening in slow motion and now people are packing up and going away faster than we can keep tabs on them.'

'Well, I'm not going anywhere, as you very well know.'

Don grinned. 'Good old reliable Charlotte.'

'You make me sound like a paddle steamer or a tank,' she protested. 'Not so many weeks ago, you hinted I was being a bit flighty, going to see the Flying Circus.'

'I was worried, that's all. I knew how Robert felt about my little sister and I didn't want to see things get in a muddle. Philip the Pilot obviously has a girl in every town.'

'Not these days, I fancy. Come to think of it, Robert and me courting is another thing that's happened in a hurry,' she said, her face troubled. 'Don, you don't think Robert's feelings for me are simply because of this war, do you? I don't think I could bear that.'

'I wish you wouldn't talk such tosh,' said Don. 'Some fellows are playing the emotional card but I can assure you, he's not that kind of person. He hasn't said as much to me but I suspect he's been waiting for you to grow into a woman. Two years is quite a long time and when he was eighteen and you were sixteen, he probably didn't feel the time was right.'

'Pearl was only saying to me today how everyone thought I'd had to grow up fast after we lost Mum.'

'Did she say that? Good for her. I do like that young woman.'

'Well, I wish you'd flipping well tell her so.'

He stuck his hands on his hips and glowered at his sister. 'I'm about to do that very thing this evening, once I've done my duty and said nice things to Auntie Eleanor. I want to call on Pearl then meet Robert for a drink afterwards.'

'Whoopee,' yelled Charlotte. 'I'm delighted you've made up your mind and even more delighted you're calling on Pearl before you go drinking beer with Robert.'

She heard a knock at the front door. 'Will you go? It's sure to be Eleanor.'

Don cocked an ear. 'Sounds like Dad's already beaten me to it.'

Charlotte stared at her brother. 'Sounds like maybe I should come round to Pearl's with you later. I could be jumping to conclusions, but I can't help feeling I might be left playing gooseberry once you've gone out.'

She watched her brother's jaw drop. Sometimes it was good to be first to find something out before he did.

★   ★   ★

'It's a lovely room, Charlotte. I hope you haven't gone to a lot of trouble. I'm supposed to be saving you from too much housework, not the reverse.'

Charlotte smoothed the jade green candlewick bedspread. 'I've always thought this room should be used more. It's directly above the kitchen so I reckon it's never too cold in here.' She pointed to a single bar electric fire. 'When you need a bit of extra warmth, you can switch this on of course.'

'Thank you. Is it all right if I use that

big wardrobe? I'd like to bring a few changes of clothing with me.'

'Of course it's all right. I want you to think of this house as your temporary home.' Impetuously she turned round and gave Eleanor a hug.

'That's very kind, Charlotte. By the way, I'm never sure whether you like to be called by your full name or whether nowadays you prefer Charlie.'

'I answer to both. Mum and Dad always called me by my full name.' She put her head on one side. 'Come to think of it, it's funny how I'm Charlie to Pearl but mostly Charlotte to Robert and they're both friends and not family.'

'Don calls you Charlie, I notice.'

'Amongst other things,' Charlotte made a face. 'Some of them aren't very polite but then he is my brother.'

'I think I shall go on using your given name, then,' said Eleanor. 'It's charming and you're much too feminine for me to think of you as Charlie.'

'Maybe you'll change your mind

once I come down to breakfast in my dungarees?'

'Not a chance,' Eleanor said briskly. 'Now, I don't want to take up your evening, talking about practicalities. Nor do I want you to feel I'm invading your kitchen. We'll do this your way, my dear. You're in charge.'

'Oh, no,' said Charlotte. 'We'll do this as a team and I'm delighted to be relieved of most of my domestic tasks. Why don't we wait to discuss it 'til after the men have gone away? I'm sure we can work things out as we go along. I'm sorry if it means you're going to be landed with more waiting in queues than I am.'

'I'd rather stand in a queue than tackle a petrol pump,' said Eleanor. 'I'm happy to deal with the ration books, though.'

'That suits me very well,' said Charlotte. 'I'll have petrol coupons to keep tally of before long — with a little help from Robert's mum, thank goodness.'

'It's going to be a joint effort,' said Eleanor. 'The Corner Garage team will be hard to beat. You mark my words.'

They walked downstairs together. Both Mr Moore and Don rose to their feet as the women entered the kitchen. Tempted to make a mock salute, Charlotte suppressed a grin, remembering she was on her best behaviour.

'How about a drop of sherry?' Mr Moore already had glasses and a bottle on the table.

He indicated a chair for Eleanor to sit on and Charlotte noticed he'd offered his own, rather than the fourth one which normally stood empty. The tiny tactful gesture touched her and she was forced to swallow hard. Her father would never look to replace her mum but if he and Eleanor had formed some kind of understanding, she appreciated the low-key way they were going about it.

'Not for me, Dad, thanks.' Don remained on his feet. 'If you and Auntie Eleanor have no objection, I'll go and pay a couple of visits.'

'Don't hang around on my account, Donald,' said Eleanor, accepting a glass of sherry. 'And isn't it time you dropped the auntie? Thank you, Raymond.'

'I'll pour a very small measure for you, son,' said Mr Moore. 'I want to propose a toast before you slope off.'

He handed glasses to Charlotte and Don then raised his own glass. 'Here's to old friends and new beginnings,' he said. 'May the British people remain resolute and hold their heads high. And may we and our loved ones be reunited before too long.' He looked at Don, Charlotte and Eleanor in turn. 'Here's to Victory.'

'To Victory,' repeated the others.

They sipped their sherry in silence, Charlotte's thoughts turning to Robert. She longed to ask Don if she could tag along but knew that wouldn't be fair. The two young men had been friends ever since the Costello family moved into the town and Robert joined Don's class at school. Besides, her brother wanted to call on Pearl and say his piece. She didn't want to interfere with that after wishing he'd get on with things. If Pearl obtained the job she wanted, she'd be mixing with lots of people in her own age group, service-men as well as women. If she really had feelings for Don, she could be sure of his loyalty to her. Donald Moore might have taken a while to get around to it but at last he seemed to see Pearl not as his sister's pigtailed schoolmate but as a lovely young woman with a sense of responsibility and her sights set on the future.

Charlotte concentrated on her dad and Eleanor's conversation. Mr Moore had fetched a couple of old photograph albums and they were talking about old times.

Eleanor pointed to one of the snaps. 'I remember that motor club dance very clearly — even smell the lilies in that big arrangement! Noelene and I were determined to get you on the dance floor. We had a little bet on which one of us would succeed, if I recall.'

'How the heck can you remember that?' Mr Moore's brow creased. 'There were quite a few dances at Randalls. I was never too keen on tripping the light fantastic.'

Eleanor smiled at Charlotte. 'That was only the second one I'd been to and I remember my dress. It was royal blue with frills and I thought I was the bee's knees. Your mother was the belle of the ball though. She wore a dress that changed from green to blue and back again as she moved.' She smiled at Mr Moore. 'The Johnson boy had his eye on her but you cut in and the rest is history!'

Watching the two of them smile at one another, Charlie thought how good it was, seeing her father look so animated and talking to someone his own age. How strange that this autumn relationship should appear to blossom just as her dad was about to re-enlist in the Army. He could have opted to stay home and no doubt quietly court Eleanor. But he wasn't that kind of person. I'm very proud of my dad too, Mum, were Charlotte's unsaid words.

★   ★   ★

Charlotte was sitting quietly, reading her library book, when her father returned from escorting Eleanor back to her flat above the hairdressing salon.

'Shall we have a cup of cocoa, love?' Mr Moore rubbed his hands together and stood close to the stove. 'I'll make it.'

'No, let me,' she said, putting down her book. 'You were quick.'

'I saw Eleanor to her door and came straight back.' He rubbed his chin and glanced at his daughter. 'I wouldn't want you to think I was being disloyal to your mother's memory.'

'I don't think any such thing, Dad.' Charlotte placed a pan of milk on top of the stove.

'El's been a good friend over the years.'

'She's always been part of my life and she was kindness itself during Mum's illness . . . and, afterwards. I'll never forget that,' said Charlotte quietly.

'You and your brother have kept me going. But over the last few months I've been thinking hard about the future.' He sat down at the kitchen table. 'I think I made the right decision about joining up again. But I realise I handed you a bit of an ultimatum. You may have had thoughts of your own about volunteering and moving away. Seeing what life's like away from Peel Bay.'

'No,' Charlie said. 'My staying here to look after things is the right decision too. And ever since Robert and I became close and you've organised a team to help keep me in order, I'm pleased I'll be able to keep an eye on his parents for him. Now,' she shot a wicked grin at her dad, 'it seems I'll be keeping an eye on Eleanor for you as well.'

'Keep an eye on that pan too, love,' he said. 'And thank you for saying what you did. We have to jog along now and hope for the best. Do you reckon you can get on all right with your godmother?'

Charlotte stirred hot milk into two cups. 'I see no reason why not. We'll have the domestic routine to talk about as well as what we hear on the radio. She enjoys reading too. We might even venture to the cinema now and then, to cheer ourselves up.'

'You'll need to keep your wits about you. Keep your eyes peeled for any funny business. War brings out the best in some people — the dark side in others.'

Charlie's hand trembled as she put her dad's cup down on the table. 'In that case, I'm extra glad Mr Costello's going to be around. I imagine he must have a good nose for odd goings-on.' She turned her head. 'That's Don back. I doubt he'll be wanting cocoa if he's been drinking beer.'

'If I know your brother, he'll be after a snack.'

Don pushed open the door. 'Any chance of a bit of bread and cheese? I'm still a growing lad.'

Charlotte watched her dad throw back his head and roar with laughter. She was going to miss these two so much. She knew she'd miss Robert of course but she'd known no other life than the one lived in the family home. Now she realised how wise was her father's decision to suggest Eleanor should move in. Having someone to share a laugh with, as well as day-to-day chores, would prove vital.

'How was Robert?' Charlie tried to appear nonchalant.

Don winked at his father. 'Robert? I reckon he was out with another woman!'

Charlotte folded her arms. 'Not even bread and water for you then, brother dear.'

Don held up his arms in surrender. 'Only joking.' He fished in his pocket and produced a small brown envelope. 'Trade you this for a bit of supper?'

She whipped the letter from his hand and tucked it in her pocket. 'Seeing as I won't be feeding you much longer, I'll make you a sandwich.'

'Aren't you going to open your love letter, sis?'

'Come on, Don. If you want to talk about romance, why don't you stand up and be counted?'

Years later, Charlotte would remember that moment — the moment when she, her brother and indeed her father, stood on the brink of three different love stories. Years later, she would remember the trials and tribulations each of them would undergo in order to find contentment with the object of their affection.

★   ★   ★

Once upstairs, Charlotte ripped open her envelope and took out a small sheet of flimsy lined paper. Robert's taste, or more likely his mother's, obviously didn't run to fancy stationery. She held the letter against her chest, wondering what he had to say, savouring the feeling of anticipation. After all, despite her brother's joking, this truly might be her very first love letter and she'd no intention of rushing such a precious and magical moment.

Yet as she began reading the brief message, it was as if someone reached inside her chest and squeezed her heart, robbing her breath, her hopes and her happiness. The young man she loved surely couldn't have written the words on this page?

Charlotte lay back on her pale pink eiderdown and buried her face in her hands, muffled sobs wracking her body. What, oh what, had brought this on? Now she faced a night's tossing and turning, wondering what she'd done to deserve this polite little epistle. He said he wanted to see her before he left for training camp. Tomorrow morning she and her father had an appointment with their bank manager. It was something to do with her ability to sign cheques in the garage proprietor's absence. She'd ask her father to drop her over at the fun fair afterwards so she could make sense of the rubbish Robert seemed to have in his head. It hurt, discovering how he could undervalue her feelings for him. Suddenly, convincing him otherwise had become the most important thing in the world.

* * *

'I'll drop you off round the back,' her father said as he drove along the old harbour road.

'Are you sure? I could walk from here.' She knew he'd a million things to do before he left Peel Bay.

'Certain. I've begun handing over the reins today. We've got you sorted out with the bank and I left George and Jack to have some instruction from Don. They certainly don't need me hovering over them.'

For a moment she thought he was about to add something else but it wasn't in his nature to reveal his emotions.

'Eleanor and I will be all right, Dad,' she said. 'I know we'll come through this OK. All of us.'

He smiled at her. 'I hope you're right, my girl. Now, off you go to that young man of yours. You'll be back by half-past twelve?'

'Of course. There's a pot of lentil soup sitting on the stove. See you later, Dad.'

Lunchtime cover was important. Her father and brother each took half an hour for their meal and she fitted in with them, depending which hat she wore that day. Charlotte knew she must be punctual. In future of course, she'd be sharing duties with Mr Costello. Jack, anxious as he was to become the best ever apprentice, wouldn't be allowed near the office until he'd proved his worth.

They drove slowly along the promenade where two or three walkers were enjoying the fresh air. Everywhere else seemed deserted, including the pleasure park. Her father stopped to let her out and she stood, watching the kingfisher-blue Vauxhall with its silver trim and black running boards set off before she turned to the small side door to the funfair. Soon the site would be totally barricaded, secured against winter storms and who knew what else? Charlotte slid the bolt across and lifted the latch to let herself in.

It seemed odd to see the big brassy barrel organ permanently silenced and the children's roundabouts motionless. How long would this war take? Would some of those kiddies who'd recently enjoyed the rides be too big to fit in the brightly painted cars and miniature carriages once the funfair returned to normal business? If it ever did, she thought with a pang of sadness. Robert seemed to have lost his optimism about more than one matter.

'Charlotte! How did you know I was over here? My mother's gone to help clean the church.'

'I tried the side gate. Your father's at the garage so I put two and two together.' She smiled shyly at Robert as he emerged from behind the swing boats. 'Why were you hiding behind there?'

'Everything has to be battened down. Just at the time when we should be doing our best to renovate this business ready for next year, the war has to come along and ruin everything.'

Somehow she knew he didn't need soothing remarks and platitudes. This was a young man grieving for several reasons.

'You know how sorry I am, Robert.'

He managed a faint smile and looked her up and down. 'You're dressed up posh today. I don't think I've seen you wearing a costume before.'

She looked down at her sapphire blue tweed two-piece suit, unaware how much the nipped-in jacket and box pleated skirt suited her curvy figure.

'Dad made an appointment with the

bank manager. I had to be vetted.' She wrinkled her nose.

'What's the matter?'

She shrugged. 'It makes it all seem so final — everything cut and dried like this. The other thing is, I keep saying Eleanor and I'll manage, but what if I do something wrong? Make some awful bloomer and ruin the business?' It was the first time she'd confided her innermost fears to anyone. 'I know your dad's going to be around but in the end it's down to me, isn't it?'

Robert moved a step closer. The breeze blew a lock of fair hair across Charlotte's face and he reached to trap it between his forefinger and thumb.

'Oh!' She didn't pull away, even though he'd surprised her.

'Charlotte, I . . . ' His hand dropped to his side. 'I'm so sorry.'

'Sorry about what, exactly? Sorry you don't seem able to trust me?' She held her breath, relieved she'd come out with her hurt, sarcastic comment but fearful she'd somehow unlocked Pandora's boxful of woes.

'I'm sorry about lots of things. I'm sorry and I'm angry all at the same time.' He folded his arms across his chest and looked away from her, frowning at the desolate fairground, seemingly unable to look her in the eye.

'I couldn't believe it, when I read your letter,' she whispered.

'I shouldn't have mouthed out about wanting you to wait for me. I can't go away, expecting you not to go out and enjoy yourself while you have the chance. I can't expect you to hang around for someone like me.'

'Someone like you? You don't want me, do you Robert? Isn't that what this is all about? For goodness sake, stop shilly-shallying and have the decency to tell me to my face!'

Regret and resignation showed in his expression as he turned to face her. A breeze rattled the metal loops securing the flag fluttering at the top of the flagpole, making little chinking sounds.

'I don't think I'm good enough for you, Charlotte. I've gone from being heir to a business with potential to . . . to being heir to nothing. Not to mention the fact your father's had to rescue mine, in order to keep the Costellos from going totally under.'

'What on earth brought all this on? Your mum and dad have a nice home. She's planning to offer people bed and breakfast but we know that needs time to develop. My dad needs someone to help him out of a jam. What is your problem?'

'You deserve better than the likes of me. But your dad thinks the world of you so he's handed my father a job to please you.'

'That's just where you're wrong, Mr Clever Sticks! My dad told me he knew of four men he thought suitable for the garage. He decided to go for his first choice. You know what? Your dad was that first choice. And I've heard my dad say nothing but good things about either of you — any of you! Dad said I needed to make my own decisions and to consult Mr Costello whenever I needed. That's how much confidence he has in him. As for this decision you've come to, you obviously didn't feel you should consult me. Do my feelings mean so little to you, Robert?' She dropped her voice. 'You certainly had me fooled.'

'That's not fair. I do care about you, Charlotte. I care more than you know. That's why I think it's best we remain good friends, rather than you be tied to a lowly squaddie with no prospects.'

She blew her top. 'I will not be told what to do, Robert Costello. I will not be fobbed off by silly excuses that don't add up. You must think I'm some little milksop with her head in the clouds! Well, I have news for you.'

Rerunning their encounter later in her thoughts, she wouldn't be able to recall exactly how she found herself in Robert's arms. But suddenly the two of them were clinging to one another, hugging as if they couldn't bear ever to let go. She lifted her face to his as he looked down at her.

'I want to kiss you, Charlotte.' His words were almost drowned by a noisy seagull squawking above them.

Her heart beat faster than it should. All thoughts of war and separation vanished like Cinderella's sequins at midnight. She wanted the reassurance of his kiss but daren't voice her thoughts.

Charlotte closed her eyes and let Robert Costello become the first young man ever to give her a proper, grown-up kiss. It didn't last long but his lips felt soft and warm on hers and his strong arms comforted her, making her feel cherished.

She hadn't finished with him yet.

'Now tell me you don't want me to be your girlfriend.' She tilted her chin and fixed him with a glare.

He laughed then . . . laughed and hugged her against him again. 'I've been listening to my demons,' he said, his mouth so close she could feel his breath warm on her cheek. 'It must be the heebie-jeebies about going to war. I'm sorry to have upset you, Charlotte. Do you really, truly want to wait for me? Even though I've been such an idiot?'

But she didn't reply. This time, the garage proprietor's daughter silenced him with a kiss. Neither moved away until an aircraft roared far above them, on the flight path to nearby RAF Kimberley. The sound broke the spell, bringing them back to the present.

'I must get back,' she said.

He nodded. 'I understand. Duty calls. May I see you later?' Robert's eyes were tender as he gazed at her.

She hoisted her shoulder bag higher. 'And risk another telling off?' She tried to keep her tone light but to her ears her voice sounded shaky.

He laughed. 'What do you think?'

She hesitated. 'I want to see you, of course I do. But it's your last evening, yours and Don's. Shouldn't you each be with your families?'

He took her hands in his. 'You're so thoughtful. That's one of the reasons I love you,' he said, almost as though thinking aloud.

'Say that again!' Charlotte could hardly believe what she'd heard.

'You're so thoughtful,' said Robert.

'No, Robert, I mean the other bit. I love you, I mean.'

'I love you too, Charlotte. One day, I want us to be together for always. You know what I'm saying? But for now, I'll write as often as I can.'

'You'd better,' she said, trying not to become overwhelmed with joy. 'Especially as you've discovered what I'm like when I get cross.'

'Come to the station tomorrow and see me off? Mum says she can't bear to wave goodbye.'

Charlotte took a deep breath. 'You try and keep me away. I want the last thing you see to be me waving to you. And when you come back on leave, I intend to be the first person you see standing on the platform.'

157

Charlotte in Charge

Saying goodbye to Don next day proved almost as painful as saying goodbye to Robert. Pearl and Charlotte stood, a few feet away from each other on the platform as the train slowly pulled away, taking the rookie soldiers to their new life. Charlotte suspected her friend must be lost in her own little world, as she herself was.

'I'm glad they're travelling together,' said Pearl as the two girls walked from the station towards where Charlotte had parked the car. Mr Moore wanted to spend his last day as a civilian, doing what he always did which mainly involved making sure his customers were looked after properly. He and Charlotte were to have a quiet meal together that evening with an open invitation to call round at Eleanor's flat later, if they wished. Charlotte excused herself from going, saying she wanted to tidy Don's bedroom, in reality feeling it would be good for her father to spend a quiet hour alone with his old friend.

'Well, you know you're most welcome to change your mind,' Eleanor had said.

Charlotte dropped Pearl at her house then drove home, parking her dad's Vauxhall carefully in its usual place. On the forecourt, George Costello, dressed in overalls, was serving a customer. Through the workshop door Charlotte saw her father watching young Jack mend a puncture. She'd worn her smart suit to drive to the station and needed to change into her work clothes before continuing with her day.

She let herself into the house and ran upstairs to her room. She'd made her bed neatly before driving the others to the station but now something caught her eye and she paused as she undid the dark blue buttons of her jacket. On her lace-trimmed pillow lay a cream envelope. Beside it was a brown paper bag, which she opened, only to find two bars of her favourite chocolate plus a plain white postcard with her name scrawled on the address side. The message from her brother was brief and instructed her not to eat the treat all at once and to keep her powder dry.

Tears welled but she blinked hard and picked up the envelope, looking round for the paper knife she kept on her chest of drawers. This note from Robert was as different as could possibly be from his previous letter. Although equally brief, this message filled her with joy, fuelling her determination to tackle everything lying ahead.

By the time you read this, I'll have left Peel Bay. Being parted from you won't be easy but every day that passes will bring us one day closer to seeing each other again. I love you, Charlotte, with all my heart.

He'd signed his name with a big curly capital R and added three lopsided kisses. She smiled as she imagined him asking his mother if she could find him some stationery more suitable to write a love letter upon than the thin sheet of lined paper Charlotte had last night torn into shreds and watched burst into flames in the stove.

She was determined to stay positive. She mopped up the tears signalling a poignant mix of sadness and happiness then changed swiftly into a woolly jumper and old skirt before going to collect Don's washing. Walking into her brother's room was like taking a step back into his childhood. He still kept a couple of toy tin cars on a shelf and a pile of comic books beneath his bed. A cricket bat with a grass stain left over from summer stood propped against the wall beside the wardrobe that always seemed to list to one side.

His discarded clothing, in a heap on the floor, prompted a wry smile as she gazed at the grey socks, striped shirt and Fair Isle pullover he'd worn the previous evening. It would be khaki for her big brother from now on. The trainee soldiers weren't permitted to take civilian clothing with them. At least they didn't have heavy suitcases to lug around, her brother had joked.

She wondered what Don and Robert would look like in uniform. How long would they remain at the Deaconsbury camp before the two friends were parted? Her father would be stationed not quite so far up country, at a training centre called Huddlesham. She could probably drive there in less than two hours but he would take the train next morning and be met at the other end. Saying goodbye to her dad would, she knew, sorely test her but then, he probably felt the same way. At least she'd be in familiar surroundings and not leaping into the unknown.

She felt a rush of relief as she thought of Eleanor, arriving tomorrow evening, after she'd closed the salon. An empty house would be intolerable at this time. How had she ever imagined her idea of bliss would be oceans of peace and quiet with no dirty socks smirking from the laundry basket and no meals to prepare!

* * *

Charlotte had enough cold beef left over to make a cottage pie and in spite of her churned up emotions, found she'd developed an appetite. Her father insisted they had a glass of sherry together by the living room fire before they ate. After their meal, she shooed him off round to Eleanor's place where she knew he'd be presented with one of his favourites — a rich fruitcake ready for him to take next day.

'Don't forget to give Eleanor the spare key,' Charlotte called as he put on his coat and flat tweed cap. 'You never know, I might be out delivering a can of petrol to some stranded motorist when she arrives and I don't like leaving my house key lying around.'

Mr Moore returned from his evening outing bearing a perfectly packaged cake and in sparkling form. Charlotte was determined to talk about anything but her father's imminent departure so the bedtime cocoa routine happened earlier than usual, with the unspoken agreement that an early night would be a good thing

They needed to get a move on next morning and Charlotte, ignoring the lump in her throat, made another trip to the station where, determined to remain cheerful, she waved goodbye to her father, trotting along the platform for as long as she could. The sight of her, blonde curls bouncing round her face, brought smiles to the faces of everyone in her father's compartment and instead of shedding a tear or two she found herself giggling helplessly as she waved a fond farewell to her dad and five total strangers.

Back home, she decided to put the remainder of Don's abandoned clothing in to soak then go round to the garage and see how George Costello and Jack were coping. Almost through the door, she decided George could probably do with a cup of tea and she daren't leave Jack out either. Smiling to herself, she filled the kettle and lifted it on to the ring. Some things didn't change and if keeping the flag flying and the home fires burning were important factors to remember, then so was the provision of a hot, strong cuppa.

Back at the garage, Charlotte found Robert's dad and Jack in the workshop. The young apprentice was putting a battery on charge and looked up eagerly as she appeared in the doorway, balancing the old tin tray enamelled with red poppies that, although dented, was what they always used for the tea run.

'How are you getting on?' She put down the tray on the workbench, shifting a cardboard box of screws to make room. It was always a mystery to her how anyone found anything once the tools and sundry items needed to keep a vehicle roadworthy were scattered all over the place.

'So far, so good,' said Jack. 'Thank you, Charlie.' He hesitated. 'It is all right to call you Charlie, I hope?'

'Of course it is, Jack. I'm only sorry you're having to grow up in a hurry but looking on the bright side, you're learning a trade and earning a bob or two.'

'Yes, Miss. Sorry, Miss, um, Charlie.'

She caught George's eye and laughed as the lad blushed. 'Sorry, Jack. I shouldn't laugh at you. We're all learning new things and getting to know new people. We'll get there in the end, I'm sure.'

George's attention seemed to be elsewhere, his head cocked to one side. She heard a car pull on to the forecourt but George was on his way before she could move. The aches and pains Robert had worried would cause his father problems didn't seem to be troubling Mr Costello at the moment. Long may that continue, thought

Charlotte as she pointed out the ginger biscuits to Jack.

'This won't happen every day,' she warned. 'Rationing's going to make sure of that.'

'Hello, Charlotte,' called a familiar voice.

She turned to face the open door where Mr Graham stood smiling at her.

'Is everything all right?'

'My goodness, yes. Your new mechanic told me he detected something not to his liking as I drove up the road. Turns out Ophelia needs a new fan belt! He's probably saved me a lot of inconvenience considering I'm taking the wife to see her sister tomorrow.'

Charlotte's lips twitched. It was fortunate she knew their customer called his car by a pet name. 'My father thinks a lot of George Costello,' she said. 'He'll be pleased he's got off to a good start.'

Mr Graham nodded. 'So it's you, George and Jack holding the fort, ay?'

'Not forgetting Mrs Costello who'll

be helping with the paperwork side. Pearl who normally does the books for us, is off soon to a new job at RAF Kimberley.'

The corners of Mr Graham's mouth drooped. 'With your dad, your brother and your friend all having to leave you, things won't be easy. But you're a hard worker. You'll come through, of that I'm sure.'

Charlotte hesitated but didn't point out Robert's name should be added to the list. She didn't feel abandoned by her family and friends. She felt proud to be where she was and proud of them too, for rising to the challenge. There'd be tricky times to come but woe betide anyone who didn't think she could handle whatever was thrown at her. Her inner qualms about her abilities were personal and wouldn't be voiced to anybody except maybe Eleanor.

Mr Graham signed his customer card and drove off with a cheerful wave. Charlotte, with a hundred and one things on her mind, went into the office to check there was enough change in the till. Counting the takings and going to the bank was at least one duty she was accustomed to handling.

* * *

When George and Jack left at six o'clock that evening and Charlotte checked all was secure before locking the side door behind her, it seemed strange to think of someone else being in the kitchen at this time of day. But she welcomed the smell of food cooking.

'Hello,' called Eleanor as Charlie let herself in. 'I've got a meat pie in the oven.

'I can tell. You must have worked fast.'

'I rubbed up the pastry this morning and left it in the bowl. What I need is to get used to this big monster of a stove after my little one.' She smiled at Charlotte. 'How did you enjoy being in charge for the first time?'

Charlie yawned and stretched both arms above her head. 'Oh, sorry, Eleanor. I think things must be catching up on me. Today was fine, thanks. Robert's dad looks as if working in a garage comes easily to him.'

'Good. What about the lad?'

'Jack's anxious to please. We'll see how he does when the gloss wears off.' She began unlacing her shoes. 'I'll go up and have a wash if you don't want me for anything.'

'I think it's all in hand. I've been listening to the Home Service. Your set's a big improvement on mine as well as your stove.'

'Well if you get fed up with the wireless, I've got plenty of records. I know you like Bing but there are plenty of big bands as well.' Charlotte headed for the door. 'Gosh, all of a sudden I'm starving.'

'Good,' said Eleanor. 'I reckon we can eat in twenty minutes.'

How long would it be, wondered Charlotte as she headed upstairs, before she and Eleanor might cross swords. Her godmother might have been in Charlotte's life forever but this sudden close proximity was unusual. Then, these were unusual times, she told herself. If only her mother was still alive. She'd have still been doing the bookkeeping as well as looking after the household side. They could still have taken on George Costello and Jack and things would have been sorted out.

A little voice in her head told her not to conjure up possible problems where none existed. Eleanor was giving up her comfortable flat to stay with her. If they got on well, that would be a bonus. But if they didn't, Charlotte wouldn't be afraid to suggest her godmother moved out again. *Every problem has a solution* was something her mum used to say. Worth remembering, thought Charlotte as she wriggled out of her dungarees.

'I wonder what our soldiers are having for their tea,' said Eleanor as the two women tucked into meat pie, boiled potatoes and cabbage a little later.

Charlotte and Robert had never shared a meal together because their time together as a couple had been ridiculously short. Now she pictured him sitting at a long table in a canteen, knife and fork at the ready while he demolished maybe sausages and mash and carrots. 'I expect we'll hear soon when one of them gets round to dropping us a line,' she said. 'Don's a bit of a gannet. Food will be very high on his list of priorities.'

Eleanor drank some water then put her glass down with a little thump. 'Sorry. I didn't mean to do that,' she said, her voice sounding breathless. 'It's just that we haven't talked about letter writing.'

Charlotte frowned, fork midway to her mouth. 'What is there to discuss?'

'Well,' said Eleanor. 'You'll be writing lots of letters to Robert, I imagine.'

'Of course. I expect I'll write once a week to Dad and Don as well. You know Pearl's going to write to Don, don't you? I'm very pleased about those two getting together.'

Eleanor nodded. 'Raymond told me how upset Don was when that other girl let him down so badly. I don't think Don will be expecting to receive any letters from yours truly but I know your father will be.'

Charlotte stared across the table, her thoughts whirling. 'I hadn't given it much attention, to be honest.'

'Your dad will be longing to hear how you're all getting on with the business,' Eleanor said softly. 'I can't possibly tell him much about that side of things.'

'I see what you mean,' Charlie said. 'We don't want to be saying the same things in our letters so if I stick to details about the garage and the customers and how the men are coping, you don't need to mention the business at all.'

Eleanor smiled. 'You're the boss. You'll do a far better reporting job than I could even dream of. He won't be interested in how many customers' heads I've permed but I expect he'll be glad to hear how other traders are doing. Not to mention whether you and I have bitten one another's heads off.' She shot Charlotte a quizzical glance.

Charlotte lifted her chin. 'We'd better make sure that doesn't happen, then.' She hesitated. 'I think back now and then to when Mum was alive. She and I got on pretty well, you know.'

'I do know,' said Eleanor. 'She was forever singing your praises.'

'Really? Charlotte slowly shook her head. 'She kept trying hard to coax me into doing things like dancing lessons or taking up embroidery. Fortunately I did let her teach me how to cook basic meals. I could be stubborn sometimes.'

'I can assure you she was well aware your heart belonged under a car's bonnet rather than inside a sewing box. She was convinced you'd be running the garage one day, in partnership with your husband and Donald.'

Charlotte's mouth became a round O

of surprise. 'I've never ever thought about it. Don's not said a word to me.'

'Of course not. Nor would he be thinking about it at this time. We none of us know what the future holds.'

Charlotte took advantage of the moment and placed both elbows on the table, propping her chin in her hands.

'Thanks for saying that, about Mum's thoughts, I mean. Sometimes if I got in a mood, I'd snap at her. I wish now I never had.' She sighed. 'I wonder what she'd have thought of Robert.'

'She knew him, didn't she? As Don's greatest friend?' Eleanor rose and removed their plates.

Charlotte nodded, watching her god-mother ladle stewed plums into two bowls. She got up and grabbed a tea towel, wrapping it round the handle of the custard jug standing at the back of the stove.

'I hardly took any notice of Robert in those days,' she said. 'I can vaguely remember him helping around the rides when Mum took Pearl and me down to the fair. But that wasn't often and then the day came when we decided we were too grown up for roundabouts.' She pulled a face. 'Dad put his foot down and decided we weren't old enough to be allowed into the amusement arcade on our own. Then came the Girl Guide years.'

'I can remember you in your blue uniform.' Eleanor helped herself to custard and passed the jug across the table. 'You seemed to have plenty of badges.'

'I liked the outdoor things best of all. But I did try hard. Looking back, I think I liked to please the grown-ups.' She chuckled. 'Not all the time, though!'

'I always envied your mother, having such a lovely family.'

'Nothing lovely about Don,' Charlotte said. 'Or me for that matter.'

Eleanor ignored the interruption. 'A family of my own wasn't to be. That's one of the reasons I agreed to Raymond's suggestion that I move in

176

here with you. Your mother and father were good to me, especially when Stephen didn't come back from Normandy.'

'I'm so very sorry. This rotten war must bring back lots of memories for you.'

'For many people,' Eleanor nodded. 'But this is a different era. The trench warfare was horrific. Nobody wants that kind of thing to happen again.' She rested her spoon in her bowl. 'What I'm trying to say, my dear, is I'm not trying to take your mother's place. Not that I ever could — but I think I need to make that clear to you. What I intend to do is support you every way I can. I believe Noelene would have wanted that. So if I do something to upset you and you snap at me for any reason, I shan't walk out in a huff.'

Charlotte sat back from the table. 'Ditto,' she said. 'Come to think of it, I don't know where I'd walk to.'

'Well, let's make sure it never comes to that, love. Now, I'll wash up while you go and write to that nice chap of yours.'

★   ★   ★

Three days later, the postman brought a letter card for Charlotte. She recognised the familiar handwriting immediately and tore at the perforated strips to read her father's words, realising just in time her fingers still bore the marks of the oil she'd measured and poured for the last customer.

'Bother,' she said, hearing another car pull up on the forecourt. She tucked the letter into her pocket and set off to greet whoever was outside. She'd need to wait until she could wash her hands, making sure first that Jack could take over the pumps for her. He was assisting George in the workshop and she didn't want to interrupt his training session.

As soon as she could, she rubbed her greasy hands with a cloth then visited the lavatory and rinsed her hands under the cold tap, using carbolic soap and wrinkling her nose at the same time. This wasn't her favourite smell but her father and Don would have laughed their heads off if she'd suggested placing a tablet of Camay beside the washbasin.

Charlotte peered into the workshop. Jack caught her eye. 'Do you want a break, Charlie?'

George straightened up. 'Jack's quick to learn,' he said. 'We don't want him getting a swollen head though.'

Charlotte laughed. 'No chance of that here,' she said. 'I'll pop round home and put the kettle on.' She tapped her pocket. 'Letter here from the real boss waiting to be read.'

'Our Robert's not been in touch yet,' said Mr Costello. 'His mother's on the fidget. I've told her not to fret — he'll not have a minute to himself except when he's sleeping.'

Charlotte stared at him. She longed for a letter. How could she have failed to remember Mrs Costello might too be pining for news of a certain young man? Aware of her cheeks turning pink and relieved not to be quizzed by Robert's father in front of the apprentice, Charlotte turned away. 'Tea's up in a few minutes.'

How many pots of tea will I have made for the men by the time this war's finished, she wondered. How many letters were being written at this moment to sweethearts, sons and sisters? In the meantime, news of her father would be very welcome. This evening, she'd find out whether Eleanor too was the recipient of a letter from Raymond. How strange it was to think of her godmother's heart lifting in anticipation as she, in her turn, ripped open a letter card or envelope. This war heralded change in more ways than one.

Charlotte forced herself to fill the kettle and set it upon the stove before sinking down at the kitchen table. The house was always quiet at this time of day so it didn't seem odd to be alone. By contrast, reading the words 'My dear Charlotte' seemed very strange when they were on the page in her father's (surprisingly clear for once) handwriting.

Greedily she scanned the close-written lines, looking for anything that might stand out as a major problem. She hadn't realised how protective of her father she'd become since the loss of her mother. Despite her affection for her godmother, Charlotte also looked for any hint of her father's burgeoning feelings for Eleanor. There was a brief, bread and butter reference right at the end where her father hoped she and El were finding their feet and keeping each other company.

Charlotte began at the beginning then, reading properly, smiling here and there as her father mentioned how he'd always known khaki suited him or talked about the buzz of conversation in the mess hall seeming strange after quiet meals at his own kitchen table.

He'd forgotten how partial he was to steamed marmalade pudding with custard. Then he added how much he missed the fruit pies Charlotte made and how she'd inherited her mother's light touch with pastry.

At that point she got up to warm the teapot before the kettle began to whistle. Why had he never told her that before? It was good to think she'd inherited at least one skill from her mother.

He went on to say how strange it was to sleep in a narrow bunk after years in the old double with the feather mattress. Some of the men described the Army mattresses as biscuits but her dad had been so tired the first night he'd fallen asleep quickly in the solitary cell he was allocated as a sergeant. A rather rusty sergeant, he joked in the letter.

This whole affair's going to be a real test of character, thought Charlotte folding the page up again. The war would test all of them, civilian and military, for every single one of them walked a tightrope and nobody knew who'd make it to the other side and who wouldn't.

She bit her lip. It was time to stop brooding and time to start working again. Her dad's letter brought back too many memories. She needed to look to the future and found herself thanking her lucky stars she had Eleanor to help her through the next weeks and months. Further than that, Charlotte didn't dare wonder about.

★   ★   ★

Eleanor hadn't received a letter from Raymond.

'He'll have writer's cramp if he tries to keep up with both of us at once,' she said when Charlotte asked her god-mother if she'd heard anything.

'You can read my letter,' Charlotte offered when they sat down to tea.

'No, my dear,' Eleanor said. 'I wouldn't dream of it. You can give me the gist of it though. I hope he's not too homesick.'

'It doesn't sound like it. It's a very cheerful letter but then, I don't suppose he'd want to worry either of us by sounding down in the dumps.'

Eleanor nodded. 'He's always had a cheerful nature, your dad. Even when he was away in the trenches in the last war, he always seemed matter of fact. There must be old postcards somewhere. Requests for soap, or chocolate or socks!' She smiled. 'Your mum and I tried our best to knit for our menfolk. I dread to think how many stitches we dropped while we sat chatting, needles and tongues clacking nineteen to the dozen.'

Charlotte shuddered. 'I dread to think how Robert would suffer if he had to rely on me for his socks. I hope his mum will prove better in that direction.'

'I don't mind helping out,' said Eleanor. 'I could get some wool tomorrow. I've probably got enough knitting needles to supply half the town.'

'Mum always admired your knitting skills. I've still got the little woolly cardigans you made for me. There's even a knitted dress and I must have been about ten when I last wore that.'

'A lovely shade of forget-me-not, if I remember rightly. You looked very bonny in it too. Fancy you still having that. But your mother was the expert seamstress. She could buy a remnant and whip up a creation fit for a princess.'

They sat in silence. Charlie visualised her mother's wedding dress, a short white gown Noelene had made for her wedding in 1918. Her parents had married only a week after the First World War ended. Charlotte's father had escaped relatively unscathed but of course, Eleanor's young man, Stephen, had not survived. It must have been very difficult for her, celebrating her friend's marriage while mourning her lost love. You could tell, looking at the few photographs commemorating the occasion, how sadness sat on Eleanor's shoulders even though she smiled brightly for the camera.

'You know, I think we deserve a little treat. How about taking ourselves off to the pictures on Saturday night,' said Eleanor. 'What do you reckon?'

'I reckon it's a very good idea.'

'I've lost track of what's on, I'm afraid,' said Eleanor.

'Local paper's here somewhere.' Charlotte rummaged through a pile of newspapers and magazines. 'Don was looking for an article he'd seen in one of the Sundays so the Peel Bay Gazette's ended up buried.'

'That apprentice of mine always knows what's showing. I can ask her tomorrow.'

'No, it's all right. I've found it now.' Charlotte riffled through the pages.

'Too much to hope there's a Cary Grant somewhere.'

'As it happens, you're in luck. *Bringing up Baby*'s on at the Roxy.'

'What heaven. How about you, though? Is there something you fancy?'

'Hmm, I'm not keen on Jeanette MacDonald and Nelson Eddy.' She looked at the next announcement. 'Oh dear, I think *The Dawn Patrol* would be too much like piling on the agony.'

'I agree! We need something to help keep our spirits up,' said Eleanor.

'*Rebecca of Sunnybrook Farm* is on at the Raleigh.'

'I remember your dad saying he thought Shirley Temple reminded him of you when you were eleven or so,' said Eleanor.

'Oh no! I think she seems very precocious. I hope I wasn't ever like that. Shall we opt for Cary Grant and Katherine Hepburn?'

'Let's do that,' said Eleanor. 'I'd forgotten — one of my clients saw the trailer last week. It went clean out of my mind, with the men going away and so on.'

'Did your client say it looked worth seeing?'

'She said it was hilarious, the bits she saw. Cary Grant wears a swansdown-trimmed negligee at one point.'

'Unmissable then.'

They each began to laugh.

'You see,' said Eleanor. 'Operation Cheer Up is working already.'

★   ★   ★

Next day's mail brought a letter postmarked Huddlesham. This time, Charlotte's hands were oil free as she'd been showing Robert's mother where everything was kept in the small office beyond the customer counter. Pearl was due at any moment, to go through the system with Mrs Costello, much to Charlotte's relief. It seemed a little tactless to open her letter in front of her sweetheart's mum so once again she found herself pushing an envelope inside the pocket of her trusty dungarees.

'Hey, what are you hiding away there? Come on, you can trust me!'

Pearl, cheeks pink from hurrying through a blustery morning, stood in the doorway, a big smile on her face.

'You're a sight for sore eyes, Pearl,' said Charlotte. 'I was beginning to wonder if you'd abandoned us.'

Pearl unwound her red woollen scarf. 'As if I would. I've been spending as much time as possible with my mum and dad.' A little of the sparkle faded from her brown eyes but she gave her friend a rueful smile. 'You know Mum's not been too wonderful lately?'

Charlotte nodded. 'Yes, you said. 'When is it you start work at the air base?'

'Monday. In one way I can't wait but in another, I feel so guilty, so sad about leaving home.'

'You mustn't! Feel guilty, I mean. Your mum has your dad to watch over her and I can pop in sometimes, now Eleanor's moved in and taken on the shopping and cooking.'

'How are you two getting on?'

'So far so good. Mind you, she seems

determined to feed me up. In a funny kind of way, rationing might prove to be my salvation. Otherwise, Robert might come back on leave and find I've grown twice as big in his absence.'

Pearl chuckled. 'I rather doubt that, given the way you run round here.' She paused. 'Seriously, Charlie, I'd love it if you could call and see my folks. I'll be home as often as I can but I'll probably find the first few days hard-going. Not that I'm afraid of pulling my weight,' she added defensively.

Charlotte patted her friend's arm. 'No one would ever think that of you,' she said, looking over her shoulder. 'I'll introduce you to Robert's mum now.' She lowered her voice. 'I'm sure you'll get on well. I got a letter from him today but please don't mention it. His dad says they still haven't heard so . . . well, you know.'

Pearl nodded. 'I'll be discretion itself. In other words, I know nothing!'

Love Letters and Little Pleasures

Pearl's arrival to explain the bookkeeping system provided the perfect excuse for Charlotte to grab some privacy in which to read Robert's letter. Once in the kitchen, she didn't even wait to fill the kettle from the tap but sat down in the old easy chair beside the stove, the seat her father often occupied in the evenings if he wanted to stay in the warm and listen to the wireless.

There were two whole pages.

Deaconsbury Training Camp
Sunday 10th September 1939

My dear Charlotte
I wouldn't call myself the best of correspondents so please forgive me if my sentences don't always turn out

like they should. First things first, thank you for driving us to the station and most of all thank you for saying you'll be my girl. That means such a lot to me. More than I can ever tell you.

I hope my ma and pa will help ease the way along for you and Mrs Bennett. I didn't tell them you and me want to write to each other but I'm pretty sure they've guessed. I shall drop them a line after I finish my letter to you but the kind of things I shall say to them won't be what I'll be saying to you!

Charlotte smiled to herself at that comment which she'd keep to herself, of course. She skimmed the part about accommodation, the food and one or two of the other new recruits Robert had palled up with, as he put it. She nodded with satisfaction, noting her brother had sent a postcard to Pearl. That was something she could pass on to her friend and would doubtless mean more to her than the cup of tea Charlotte was supposing to be making!

Clicking her tongue against her top row of teeth, Charlotte hurried to fill the kettle, put it to heat on the stove and picked up her precious letter again. She suspected Robert had abandoned the task halfway through, because the next section appeared slightly lighter than the first, which appeared in very bold pencil. Maybe he'd lost the first one and borrowed someone else's. It didn't matter. The sentiment behind the words was by far the most important thing.

I want you to know how much you mean to me. I want you to think of me at night when you say your prayers and remember me in them, please, my dear lovely Charlotte — as I shall remember you in mine.

It's almost time now for lights out. Before we know it it'll be time to rise and shine. That's Army life for you. Square bashing and spit and polish till the cows come home. Take very good care of yourself my dearest and don't forget to confide in my father if you have any worries or if some pesky so and so tries to make eyes at you!

Your ever-loving Robert xxx

PS If you can send me a snap of yourself it would be very much appreciated. The days seemed to go by in a rush and I should have got Don to photograph the two of us together. But far better I have one of you and not one with my ugly mug on it, I think!

Ugly mug indeed! Eleanor had teased Charlotte about her young man having matinee idol looks. He was a handsome fellow, without a doubt and it would be lovely to have a photograph of him to keep on her bedside table. Perhaps when he came home on leave, they could sort something out.

She was admiring that big curly R on his signature again when the kettle began whistling, bringing her down to earth. Tea for five people took priority over her love letter, at least for the time being.

Once the tea had brewed, Charlotte poured it carefully into a tall jug. She'd need to make two journeys to make sure she didn't tilt the tray and cause an upset. What a shame someone couldn't invent a machine for dispensing tea. If they could do it with petrol, surely they could do it for the cup that cheered?

* * *

Eleanor and Charlotte's cinema trip proved a great success.

'At least we can sit in someone else's blacked out room this evening,' said Charlotte as they made their way, arm in arm, down the road to the cinema.

'I still can't get used to it,' said Eleanor. 'The autumn days will seem extra short this year. You know that big screen I have at the salon to stop the light escaping when people come in and go out? It's really rather unstable. I need to find a way of securing it.'

Charlotte almost offered Robert's services to take a look at it but stopped in time. 'It's difficult for everyone,' she said. 'We've no option but to close the garage earlier and earlier as the evenings draw in. Just imagine if you lived in a vicarage. They're usually built to house a big family, aren't they? That must take miles of black cotton.'

'True, though I expect some of the rooms can be shut up for the duration, if nobody needs to use them.'

'I don't know what I'd have done without your help, Eleanor. Measuring up and getting the material, I mean. I wasn't too quick off the mark sorting out things at home.'

'Your dad said he managed for those few nights before he went away. But I need to make sure we can black out his window and Don's as well, ready for any leave coming their way. I'll do that as soon as I can so you needn't worry about it.'

'That's a relief. It strikes me this war's causing lots of extra work and worry. Let's hope it doesn't last for long.'

Eleanor sighed. 'I don't think we should get our hopes up regarding a swift ending. I wish I could tell you otherwise, but unfortunately, I can't. Raymond had a good understanding of the situation before he went away — far better than mine.'

They were nearing the cinema. 'It's a good job the Government decided to allow cinemas and theatres to reopen. I'm really looking forward to this film,' said Charlotte. 'And it's something to tell Robert about when I write next.'

Eleanor chuckled. 'Creeping in through the double doors then through whatever they've rigged up will seem peculiar. But it's great to be able to gaze at a big screen and forget the war for a while.'

'The newsreel's important, don't you think,' said Charlotte. 'We get lots of information that way.'

'I know,' Eleanor agreed. 'The

Government didn't take long to catch on, as you say. Can't wait to see Cary Grant.'

'I think he's spoken for, Auntie El.'

'Aw, I wouldn't really want to marry a film star. I reckon that would just be asking for trouble.'

As they made their way through the blackout precautions and into the foyer to pay for their seats at the dimly lit ticket booth, Charlotte found herself wondering whether her godmother also found this period in their lives to be unreal. Sometimes it seemed bizarre with so many men away and others joining them when their turn came. She felt like holding up her hand and yelling 'Stop' before any more harm could be done. No such luck. She'd have to play the waiting game with as much good grace as possible.

Eleanor purchased tickets and they moved into the auditorium where the usherette guided them to two middle seats, six rows back in the Stalls. Last time Charlotte visited the cinema, she'd sat in the back row feeling shy about being there with Robert. Then his arm around her shoulders had made her feel warm and cherished. Now she wondered when she'd experience that magical feeling again. Tonight he'd be in her prayers. If faith and love could get him through this and safely out the other end, Charlotte Moore was the girl to count upon.

The newsreel began. Men marched briskly across the screen. Latecomers hurried into their seats. Charlotte sat back and waited to be entertained.

'Katharine Hepburn has some stunning outfits,' whispered Eleanor soon after the star made her appearance.

'What do you think of Cary Grant in specs?'

Her godmother chuckled. 'Can't really imagine him being a palaeontologist! But I'd still like him if he wore a sack over his head.'

'Except that'd mean you couldn't gaze at his chiselled jaw.'

'Shush!' The curt command came

from the row behind.

Charlotte froze, not daring to glance sideways at Eleanor lest she burst out laughing. She lost herself in the story, loving every moment and laughing at every rib-tickling incident.

On the way home, they made their way carefully along streets made unfamiliar by the dark cloak of blackout restrictions. Their eyes had been focused upon the bright cinema screen and at first both agreed they seemed to wade through nothing but unforgiving dense darkness. Charlotte thought of the time at Fun Land when she'd pushed through those double doors of the ghost train ride, with Robert shining the torch, its beam highlighting the sham spooky effects. How much had happened since then.

At last, eyes adjusting, the two women found they could step out with more confidence. Maybe that's what it's all about, thought Charlotte. If I learn to accept the situation we're in, it will become easier as time goes by.

* * *

'When I opened up the salon this morning, I found a letter on the doormat.' Eleanor's words greeted Charlotte as she let herself into the kitchen one chill October evening.

'You mean from Dad? Is he well?'

'Very well indeed. He thinks all that running back and forth between petrol pumps and money drawer must have helped keep him fit.'

Charlotte nodded. 'My dungarees are looser than they used to be. It's no bad thing, either.'

'Well, don't loose too much weight. Rationing won't help either.'

'Most of our customers are either discussing the increase in the price of petrol or they're wondering how they're expected to manage without this, that or the other.'

Eleanor stirred the soup simmering on the hob. 'It's much the same with my clients, though they're more concerned with clothes and food coupons than petrol prices.'

'Any more news from Dad?' Charlotte didn't want to pry but she had the impression Eleanor was bursting to tell her something.

'Yes.' Her godmother's face shone with pleasure. 'He says to tell you there's a strong possibility he'll get leave over Christmas.'

Charlotte gave a little cheer, rushed over to the stove, grabbed the wooden spoon from her godmother's hand and waltzed her round the kitchen table until Eleanor begged for mercy. 'I'm not so young and energetic as you are,' she complained. 'Pooh ... Eau de Petroleum's all right in its place but I wish you'd wash your hands before you dance with me!'

Charlotte giggled. 'I shall remember in future. What a lovely bit of news, though — about Dad, I mean. It's not a bad journey to Huddlesham and back. If the weather doesn't play up, I could drive him to the camp on the morning he's due back. That'd give him some extra time.'

'Let's hope they don't want him back by midnight on Boxing Day. Christmas Day's on a Wednesday this year.' Eleanor retrieved her spoon. 'Will you open for business?'

'Oh yes,' said Charlotte. 'If only for a few hours. Customers expect it.'

'We can time the meal for early evening so we all sit down together.' She looked expectantly at Charlotte. 'If that suits you, my dear?'

'Are you volunteering to cook dinner?'

'Of course. But I wouldn't want to impose. You and Raymond and maybe even Don if he can get leave too, might prefer to spend the day as family.'

'But you're family too, Auntie El,' Charlotte's tone was indignant. 'I thought those friends you used to go to for Christmas Day had moved to York?'

'That's right.'

'So you'd be on your own if you weren't here?'

'Well, yes. I suppose so.'

'Your place is here, with your family.' Charlotte edged her way past the stove to the sink and began washing her hands.

'You don't know how happy it makes me feel to hear you say that,' said her godmother.

'I'm sure it's what Mum would've wanted. Specially after all you're doing to help us.' Charlotte scrubbed her nails vigorously.

Eleanor sank into the easy chair beside the stove and clasped her hands around her knees. 'Thank you,' she said. 'I know Raymond will always love Noelene.' She looked up at Charlotte's profile. 'I would expect nothing less. I never dreamt your father and I might become fond of one another.'

'I imagine you still love Stephen,' said Charlotte cautiously. 'Even after all those years.'

'Love is timeless, my dear. You're right when you say I still love my late fiancé. Your father and I have some shared history as you well know. We enjoy each other's company.'

Charlotte took a deep breath. 'I'm pleased. I really am. Because one day, if we're spared, I know Robert and I will marry and I'll leave home.' Her hands flew to her mouth. Wide-eyed she stared at her godmother. 'I didn't mean to say that. I hope I'm not tempting fate.'

'I'm sure you're not doing any such thing,' Eleanor said gently. 'You did take the trouble to say if you were spared. I'm delighted to hear you sound so sure of your feelings for each other and to know you're happy, Charlotte.'

'Thank you. But please don't say anything to anyone, will you? Not even to Dad. It's early days. I still feel cheated out of a proper courtship. Robert and I haven't even discussed becoming engaged yet. And if we do, it might be one of the longest ever engagements.'

Eleanor rose to rescue the soup from bubbling a tad too vigorously. 'You don't know that. When Robert has some leave, I'm sure he'll want to talk about your future together. The thought will be helping keep him strong and focused, you know. The possibility of being with the girl he loves one day.'

Charlotte nodded, trying not to let the tears well. There was so much to look forward to. In spite of the dark days and evil deeds happening in Europe and beyond, not even the threat of Hitler's big bad bombers could quench the love she felt for her young man.

★　★　★

December tested everyone's resolve, bringing not only fewer daylight hours, but also such searching cold, Charlotte's fingers and toes felt numb as she coped with working outside in freezing conditions. Eleanor knitted her a woollen cap with earflaps that she complained made her look funny but which she wore with gratitude. Customers stayed inside their cars while their tanks were filled, their breath steaming up the inside of the windows as they waited. There were petrol coupons to deal with as well as money and when her fingers fumbled while she collected the right change, Charlotte sometimes stamped her feet in frustration at the time taken. Fortunately, people understood, often speaking of the weather as another enemy to be overcome.

Late one afternoon, as Charlotte counted the takings and made sure there was enough change to start them off next day, the telephone rang. She sighed because she was counting three-penny pieces and had almost collected a pound's worth.

She picked up the receiver and said 'Corner Garage.'

'Go ahead, caller,' said the operator.

Charlotte held her breath.

'Hello, Charlotte. It's me.'

'Robert! Are you all right?'

'Yes. I'm being allowed leave. Only a few days but I'm taking the train on Friday.'

'George hasn't said anything — did you want to speak to him? He's still in the workshop.'

'You let him know for me, Charlotte, please. He can tell Ma.'

'Of course. What time's your train due in Coynesbury?'

'Two thirty if I make my connections. I can get the bus and hop off at the garage stop if you like.'

'I'll drive to Coynesbury and meet the train. I've been very careful with my petrol allowance.'

At first she wondered if he'd heard properly. Then he spoke softly. 'I want you to be the first person I see as the train pulls into the platform.'

'You remembered!'

'Did you really think I'd forget?'

Charlotte's breath caught in her throat, preventing her from finding the words to answer him.

'Are you there?' His voice sounded anxious.

'I'm still here, Robert. I can't believe I'm going to see you so soon. Will they allow you Christmas leave as well? Oh, I do hope so.'

'I'll explain it all when I see you.' He paused. 'Look, lovey, I'd better go. There's a queue of blokes behind. Ta ta for now. I'll see you on Friday.'

'Robert, I . . . ' Charlotte heard a buzzing as the connection broke. He'd gone. But soon he'd be travelling home and she'd have her first sight of him in uniform.

Charlotte's pile of three-penny pieces toppled as she abandoned coin counting and flew out of the office towards the workshop. 'George,' she called. 'You'll never guess who I've been talking to?'

Mr Costello looked up as she appeared in the doorway. He put down the rag he was using to clean an engine part and pretended to be deep in thought, his head on one side. 'I'd lay odds on it being our boy.'

'Ten out of ten! It was Robert and he's asked me to let you and his mum know he's coming home on Friday.

Sounds like the phone was in great demand so he couldn't talk for long.'

George narrowed his eyes. 'Would this be embarkation leave? Come to think of it, he probably wouldn't tell you over the phone.'

Charlotte stared at him. 'He didn't say anything much, except the bare essentials. He's going to explain everything when he gets here, I do know that much.'

Robert's father nodded, his expression grave. 'It'll be good to see the lad. His ma will be over the moon.' His face creased as he grinned at Charlotte. 'You'll need to take some time off, I reckon.'

'I can't leave you and Jack to do everything.'

'We can manage without you for a couple of days. You make the most of having your young man home, while the pair of you have the chance.'

Pleasure at the thought of spending time with Robert spread through her whole being like runny honey over warm bread but it came tinged with apprehension as she contemplated the possibility of him being sent to a war zone. Charlotte knew she must put the thought behind her. She couldn't remember the last time she took a whole day off from the business unless it was to complete some major domestic task like spring-cleaning. It wasn't the kind of holiday weather she preferred but who needed sunshine when they anticipated their sweetheart's imminent arrival?

★   ★   ★

'Mr and Mrs Costello have invited me round to tea on Robert's first evening,' said Charlotte when she arrived after work next day. 'George asked me this morning.'

'That's kind,' said Eleanor. 'So I could have a night off from cooking?'

Charlotte stiffened. 'You don't have to wait for me to go out before you take a night off. The last thing I want is for you to feel an obligation to be here every evening.'

'I know you don't,' said Eleanor, putting her hands on her hips. 'I want to ask my neighbour, Doris, round for a bite to eat some time and this seems a good opportunity.'

'So I'm stopping you from enjoying a social life, am I?'

Eleanor stared at her goddaughter. 'Are you all right, Charlotte? You're not normally so prickly. Of course you're not stopping me from having a social life. It so happens I'm not interested these days. You know your father thought it was a good idea if we teamed up for the time being.'

Charlotte stooped to unlace her work shoes. 'I'm sorry,' she mumbled. 'I'm just a bit . . . '

'Apprehensive?'

'I think I am but I don't know why I should be. I can't wait to see Robert but we haven't seen much of each other, certainly not alone. We'll be walking out together, spending time here or at his house. What if he finds me boring?'

'He won't find you boring. Tell you what, I bet he's thinking exactly the same as you. He's probably wondering what on earth you see in him, especially as he'll be wearing his uniform and sporting a short back and sides the likes of which you've never seen on him before.'

Charlotte stood there in her thick wool socks, staring at Eleanor. 'Do you really think so?'

'I do. Now, why don't you hurry upstairs and fetch those nice warm slacks of yours and your Shetland sweater. Bring them back down here and get changed by the stove. Then I think you and I need a little pick me up.'

Charlotte admitted to feeling a whole lot more cheerful once she changed into comfortable clothes and settled into the easy chair, letting her godmother pour her a glass of sherry, just for a special treat and not to make a habit of.

'Robert always seems so self-possessed,' Charlotte said after taking a sip of the rich wine. 'I know he's older than me but comparing him with my brother, he seems older than Don.'

'He's the only son and he's probably had more in his life to worry about than you and Donald have — business matters, I mean. I'm not trying to make light of your family situation, love.'

'Mum and Dad had a tough time financially when Don and I were kids, didn't they? She told me much later on how they'd felt they were constantly clinging to the edge of a precipice, worried sick the bank manager would give them an ultimatum. Lots of people have had business worries because of the depression and now the war.'

Eleanor nodded her silvery-fair head. 'You're right, of course. But you and your brother were born in Peel Bay. You've always lived here and a lot of people know you and your history. The Costello family drifted for some years, I gather, before they settled here to take over Fun Land.'

'Does that make them any worse people?'

'No, of course not,' said Eleanor. 'All I'm saying is that Robert's probably a bit more world wise than you are. He's had to cope with changing schools and being unable to maintain friendships. You're an extremely competent young woman and he probably admires that quality in you. I hardly know the boy but I don't imagine he'd be attracted to a shrinking violet type of girl.'

Charlotte collapsed into giggles. 'I shall have to watch out this sherry doesn't make me squiffy,' she said.

'You need some food inside you. Braised beef and onions tonight, with carrots and cabbage. I cheated and bought two fruit trifles from Ashton's Bakery for our pudding.'

'My favourites.' Charlotte cradled her glass between her fingers and watched the golden liquid swirl and settle. 'I'm very lucky to have you around, Auntie El. Not sure you're so lucky about the boot being on the other foot though . . . '

Her godmother laughed and began draining vegetables. 'If we have the odd falling out while all this is going on, my dear, we won't have too much to complain about.'

Charlotte rose from her cosy seat and began laying the table. 'I could have ended up on some bleak air base or Army camp in the back of beyond — fat chance I'd have had of seeing Robert then. We could've gone for years without seeing each other, couldn't we?'

Eleanor's back was turned. 'Oh, easily,' she said. 'That's why you need to treasure every precious moment while he's home on leave. Talk to one another and share your thoughts and your memories. He should be your very best friend.'

'Not Pearl?'

'I don't mean you should drop Pearl, good heavens, no. What I mean is, your husband to be should be your soul mate and your partner in every way. That's the ideal. Young women sometimes think they're in love but when it comes to it, they sometimes find they don't like the person. The same goes for men falling for women too.'

'Don and Kitty for example?'

Eleanor ladled meat and gravy on to two plates. The savoury smell filled the kitchen and Charlotte's tummy rumbled loudly.

'Time to eat,' said Eleanor. 'But yes, I know Kitty's very glamorous and I'm sure she attracts lots of attention. I imagine she fell for Donald because he's a good-looking young man working in an established family business. But she was marking time with him, not developing a real friendship.'

Charlotte waited for Eleanor to seat herself then picked up her knife and fork. 'I understand what you're saying. Don heard through the grapevine she was trying to make someone else jealous. I hate that kind of behaviour.'

Eleanor chuckled. 'Of course you do. You're not the kind of person to scheme and plot in order to get what you want. You take life on the chin, love. It's a good characteristic to have and it'll stand you in good stead for the future.' She lifted a forkful to her mouth and chewed.

'Top marks, Auntie El. This is a lovely meal. And thanks for the chat. I was starting to get a bit edgy. I'm sorry if I upset you.'

'You're a human being like the rest of us. I couldn't bear living with someone who was perfect.'

'Then you're definitely in the right place.'

Tea for Two

Tiny flecks of snow fluttered from a leaden sky as Charlotte parked her father's car then walked across to the station. Coynesbury was the market town, about fifteen miles inland from Peel Bay. She knew she'd arrived too early. She also knew she couldn't have tolerated one single minute longer at home, so eager was she to find the correct platform for the train bringing Robert back to her.

Among the shifting crowds were many servicemen and women. Charlotte enjoyed watching the faces as passengers arriving at the barrier found a loved one waiting. She looked away quickly as a nearby couple embraced, the man in his naval uniform, sweeping the woman off her feet and whirling her around in his arms. It seemed wrong to spy on their joyful reconciliation.

She was almost tempted to visit the station buffet while she watched the minutes tick away on the enormous round clock suspended above the platform. Instead she bought a newspaper and went into the ladies' waiting room, having checked with a porter she was on the correct platform.

Eleanor had said, don't chatter away nineteen to the dozen. Let Robert take the lead. He's been shut up with dozens of other young fellows for almost three months. Don't worry if it seems as though you're meeting a stranger. Don't be surprised if he's picked up expressions you don't remember him using before he joined up. He belongs to two different worlds now. You can't possibly know what he's going through but you and his parents are the constant things in his life and it's important you don't try to act too sophisticated or clever. In particular, don't talk about other men.

Charlotte had queried this, more than a little indignant because this whole business of falling in love and conducting a romance seemed so complicated. She talked to lots of men every day. Most of her customers were male and then there were the oil and tyre company representatives, as well as salesmen hoping to sell her puncture repair kits, tins of wax for polishing motor cars and all sorts of impedimenta. This was her life, she'd told her godmother.

Eleanor insisted that didn't matter. If the conversation lags, don't be afraid of silences, she said. You can always talk about Pearl. Talk about your dad's letters and how Donald's getting on at his new posting. Don't pester him with too many questions, she'd advised.

Charlotte looked at her wristwatch and jumped to her feet, panic striking as she realised the train was due in five more minutes. Her sense of humour rescued her. With any luck he'd recognise her from a distance. She was wearing an overcoat teamed with a black felt hat, pulled down over her ears. If she'd worn the woolly cap with the earflaps, he'd probably have looked straight through her.

Bracing herself, she opened the waiting room door and stepped on to the platform. Passengers stood alone or in twos and threes, suitcases or kitbags at their feet. Some blew on their hands or performed a little jig in order to keep warm. A group of airmen, doubtless from the base where Pearl worked, stood together, laughing and joking. They seemed unaffected by the bone chilling temperature, maybe buoyed up by the thought of their weekend pass and the journey to London, final destination of Robert's train. One of them was very tall, several inches taller than Charlotte. He glanced at her and smiled as she walked by. She returned his smile but continued her progress along the platform. Behind her a bubble of laughter from the RAF boys told her the tall one was probably being teased and maybe egged on to engage her in conversation.

Nothing could deter her from keeping her promise. She'd reached the end of the platform.

A porter approached, wheeling a trolley. 'You'll have to walk back, Miss, if you want to find a seat quickly. This here's where the luggage van stops.'

'It's all right, thank you, I'm meeting someone. Is there any delay?'

The man shook his head and jerked his thumb in the direction of the track. 'Train's on time.' He peered into the distance. 'Here she comes.'

At first the train was only a distant rumble then Charlotte caught sight of the engine and saw the smoke belching, heard the rumbling turning into thundering as the big locomotive dropped speed and clanked along the rails, squealing brakes adding to the noise. She began waving as soon as the steam engine whooshed past and the first carriage slid by. Faces gazed through the windows but often grime obscured the glass and all she saw was an indistinct mass. If Robert was trying to spot her, he probably had more chance than she had of identifying him. She went on waving, often being waved back to by cheerful travellers but still unsure whether Robert was actually on board or not.

When the train stopped, she began walking slowly back up the platform where passengers were disembarking and those waiting to board jostled their way towards open doors. Khaki-clad soldiers of various shapes and sizes were everywhere, toting kitbags. Charlotte stopped walking, her mittened hands clasped together as she searched in vain.

Suddenly he was there. A gap in the crowd showed him standing a few yards from her. Their gazes locked and he began hurrying towards her, his kitbag hoisted over one shoulder.

'Mind your backs,' a porter called, wheeling a loaded baggage trolley towards the exit.

Robert sidestepped the trolley and arrived in front of Charlotte. He dumped his bag at his feet and held out his arms to her. She dived into his embrace and all her doubts and nervousness melted away faster than the steam vanishing into the wintry air.

After they'd clung together for moments, seconds or minutes — Charlotte couldn't recall later — Robert kissed the tip of her nose. She smiled up at him. How tall he seemed! His uniform either made him appear incredibly young or impossibly mature. She really couldn't say which.

'You look lovely,' he said. 'Like a winter princess.'

She laughed shakily. 'Thank you. This was my mum's coat. I must be the same size now as she was.'

His eyes were tender. 'I expect she'd be pleased to know her coat was keeping you warm. Is that her hat too?'

'It's Eleanor's,' said Charlotte with a grin.

He nodded, still holding on to her hands as the crowd dispersed around them. 'I saw a figure in a pretty tweed coat and knew it was you. Two of the lads in my compartment were waving as well. I couldn't stop myself from saying you were my girl, come to meet me.'

'You've probably never seen me in a hat before.'

'You've never seen me wearing uniform before.' He let go of her hands and picked up his kit bag. 'Is there somewhere near the station where we can get a bite to eat?'

She clung to his arm and they headed for the stairs leading to the barrier. 'There's a Lyons' Corner House quite close.'

'I'd like some time alone with you, before we drive home. Is that all right, sweetheart? Do you have to get back quickly?'

She squeezed his arm through his greatcoat. 'I've been given time off for good behaviour,' she said. 'Mr Costello's orders!'

Robert laughed. He fumbled for his travel warrant as they drew near the barrier. Charlotte felt in her pocket for her platform ticket and they pushed through the turnstile, Robert ushering her ahead of him.

The café was warm, full of chattering customers and in Charlotte's eyes, the most romantic place in the world just then. If you'd offered her a trip to see Rome's Trevi Fountain or Niagara Falls, she would not have accepted unless Robert accompanied her.

They found a table for two in a corner. Robert pulled out a chair for her and she sat, unbuttoning her coat so she'd feel the benefit when they braved the December afternoon again. Robert shrugged off his greatcoat and took both their garments to a nearby hat stand. He kept his cap with him, she noticed.

'I can keep an eye on our coats from here,' he said, picking up the menu. 'Have whatever you like, Charlotte.'

'Tea for me, please. Maybe a toasted teacake would be nice. I couldn't eat much lunch, I was so excited.'

'You look as though you've lost a bit of weight. Not that you needed to,' he said.

She chuckled. 'Eleanor said much the same. Did you know she and Dad are writing to each other?'

He looked up from the menu. 'No, but I do now. It's a good thing. Everyone enjoys getting letters when they're away from home.'

She looked into the distance over his shoulder. 'The war seems to have pushed them into each other's arms. Eleanor seems very happy about it.'

'What about you?'

'What do I think about them getting together?' Her smile was wistful. 'As long as they're happy, who am I to comment? I like to see positive things coming out of this difficult situation.'

The waitress took their order then sped away again.

Robert reached round the side of the table and clasped Charlotte's hand. 'Is there something worrying you, love? Is there something you need to tell me? Have your feelings towards me changed?'

Anxiety suddenly made him look gaunt. Yet Charlotte, struck with a wave of compassion and guilt, knew for both their sakes she needed to ask him something.

'I love you, Robert,' she whispered above the clatter of crockery and buzz of conversation. 'My feelings won't ever change.'

'Then what is it? Whatever it is, we can deal with it. I don't like to think of you being worried.'

'I can't help wondering if you wanted you and me to start courting because of all the uncertainty around us. Because you knew you'd be going into the Forces. You mentioned people enjoying receiving letters.'

He shook his head in bewilderment. 'I'm the one who gave you a hard time when I asked you to make absolutely sure you wanted to be my girl. I didn't want you fretting because I wasn't around to take you to the pictures or walk hand in hand along the sands with you.' He reached inside his battledress and took out a letter. 'Here you are. I think you should read this.'

She took the envelope from him, frowning as she recognised the handwriting. Inside was one single sheet of lined notepaper, which Charlotte read quickly, read again and replaced in the envelope.

'Well?' Robert said.

'I don't know what to say.'

Amidst the chatter and clatter of the busy teashop, Robert pushed back his chair and stood up. Then he stooped beside Charlotte's chair, went down on one knee and took both her hands in his.

'You could try saying yes, my darling. Charlotte, will you do me the honour of becoming my wife?'

The room seemed to whirl before her eyes. Robert's eager, smiling face, the noise of catcalls and cheers and cries of *Oh isn't that sweet* rolled around them. She sensed the waitress hovering nearby. A wag called out, 'Go on, love, put the lad out of his misery. He wants his tea!'

Charlotte ignored everything and everyone except the man she knew she loved. 'Yes,' she whispered. 'Yes, please. Of course I'll be your wife.'

More cheers as the successful suitor gave his blushing bride to be a chaste kiss on the cheek. The waitress tactfully delivered their tray and backed away quickly. Robert returned to his chair and Charlotte busied herself with cups and saucers, wishing she wasn't wearing a hat. Bareheaded, her curls would fall forward and conceal her crimson cheeks. Hot buttered teacakes joined the silver stand of assorted fancies. Suddenly she felt very, very hungry. She'd just got engaged. Robert had written to her father to request permission to ask for her hand in marriage. What a lovely, lovely thing to do and so typical of him.

'Better now?' He watched her pour tea into his cup, her hand steady.

'Much better,' she said. 'That was such a surprise, but a wonderful one.'

'I didn't intend making a spectacle of myself,' he said. 'I was going to show you your dad's letter later. Suddenly I couldn't bear to let both of us go on wondering and waiting.' He passed her the teacakes. 'Let's eat, lovey. I'm famished.'

They didn't talk much after that. Charlotte surprised herself by eating a whole teacake then a chocolate fancy in the shape of a boat filled with delicious, squidgy coffee cream. Robert demolished everything within sight though he insisted they were well fed at camp and it was only because of his convoluted travel arrangements that he'd missed a midday meal.

After they'd wrapped themselves up again to face the elements, Robert asked her if wanted to visit a Coynesbury jeweller or whether she'd like to wait until morning and buy a ring locally.

'You don't have to spend a lot of

money,' she said. 'I'd wear a ring from Woolworths as long as it meant I was your fiancée.'

He laughed out loud as he held open the door for her. 'I think we can do a bit better than that,' he said. 'No offence to Woollies.' He glanced up at the sky. 'If it's all right with you, perhaps we should head home now. Better off not driving in the blackout if we can avoid it.'

'All right. Let's get you home,' said Charlotte.

'I'm already home, my darling.' He tucked her arm in his.

As they approached the car, she handed over the key. There were times when it was good to proclaim one's female independence. There were others when a girl wanted to feel cherished. Besides, there was a pink haze of delight surrounding her, in spite of the gloomy weather. And she didn't want to miss one moment of it by having to concentrate on driving.

Robert tucked the tartan car rug

carefully around her then swung his long legs into the car. Our first trip together as an engaged couple, thought Charlotte as the engine purred into life.

★ ★ ★

They drove past the Corner Garage on the way to Robert's house. As expected, the business was closed for the day. The snow flurry hadn't come to anything but twilight clothed the streets and no moon shed light. When Robert steered the car down the road to the old harbour, they found mist blanketing the area.

'What a welcome,' quipped Robert.

'Well, it is Peel Bay in December,' said Charlotte.

'The most wonderful place in the world right now,' he said, patting her hand.

'I think Army life's done you the world of good. You're becoming quite romantic.'

'I can't think why!' He paused. 'Yes, I

can. It's being with my new fiancée.'

'Ah, I was still plain old Charlotte when you got down on one knee,' she teased.

'You could never in a million years be described as plain old Charlotte.'

He parked the car outside his house, switched off the engine and pulled her close. She lifted her chin and their lips met.

'Peaches and cream,' he whispered when the two drew apart. 'I'd better get you inside.'

Mr and Mrs Costello were preceded to the door by an ecstatic dog. Smuggler scrambled over the doorstep, sniffed two pairs of boots and bounded back inside, barking joyfully.

Charlotte dropped to the carpet to pet the little spaniel. 'I'm sure he's grown since I saw him last,' she said, looking up at Robert's mother.

'I think my son's grown too,' said Mary Costello, giving Robert a hug then holding him at arm's length. 'You've filled out, that's what it is.'

'Square bashing, Ma, that's what it is.' Robert shook his father's hand. 'All well, Pa? You look in the pink, to me.'

'I'm enjoying my work, son.'

'I don't know what I'd do without him and Jack,' said Charlotte, scrambling to her feet.

'Well, let's go and sit by the fire,' said Mary Costello. 'We can eat when we want but you could probably do with a warm first.'

Charlotte followed her into the living room. The table was laid for a meal and a coal fire burned in the grate. She stood at the back of the room and looked round for Robert. He was at her side in a moment. As he placed his arm around her waist, Charlotte saw Mrs Costello exchange glances with her husband. She took a deep breath and waited for her brand new fiancé to break the news of the engagement to his parents.

'We have something to tell you,' he said. 'In the Coynesbury Lyons' Tea House this afternoon, I asked Charlotte to marry me.' He hugged her to him and kissed her cheek.

'That's my boy,' said George. 'With all those witnesses, you can't get out of it now, Charlie.'

'I'm really pleased for you both,' said Mary, moving to give the happy couple one big hug.

Her husband shook hands with Charlotte then looked embarrassed but delighted as his future daughter-in-law planted a kiss on his cheek.

'How about a glass of ginger wine?' George looked round at his wife.

'Good idea. You all sit down while I sort out the glasses. I'm sorry there's nothing more suitable in the house.'

'Ginger wine's lovely,' said Charlotte as Mary turned to the big sideboard. 'So's this fire. I won't want to drive home.'

'I shall drive you home later, love. I can walk back.'

'No need for that,' said Charlotte. 'If you take me home, you can drive the Vauxhall back here. That way, I'll be sure to see you tomorrow as well!'

'You can't escape me,' said Robert. He craned his neck round to address his mother. 'We're choosing the ring tomorrow. Which jeweller do you reckon is the best?'

'Pinkham's,' said Mary. 'The other place is more of a pawnbroker's. I don't think they deal in much new stuff.' She looked at Charlotte. 'Unless you'd prefer something antique?'

'I haven't really thought about it,' said Charlotte. 'Your son caught me on the hop.' She wanted to say he meant more to her than any piece of jewellery possibly could but thought the comment would make her sound too much like one of those slushy romantic movies Pearl adored.

Mr Costello held up his glass. 'Let's raise our glasses and drink to the happy couple,' he said.

'Can we join in?' Robert was grinning.

'To the happy couple,' repeated his mother.

When they'd all finished toasting one another and Charlotte was enjoying the warm, happy buzz caused by the glowing fire, the ginger wine and the affection on the Costello family's faces, they sat down to eat.

Later, sitting beside Robert while he drove her home, she rested her head on his shoulder. 'I'm so happy. Thank you,' she said.

'No, Charlotte. Thank you,' he corrected her.

'Is this our first disagreement as an engaged couple?'

'Certainly not,' he said. 'Now, tomorrow I'll be round at ten on the dot. I think we could both do with a lie in. Then it's off to the high street to buy a sparkler for your ring finger.'

'Whatever you say, Private Costello.'

★ ★ ★

In her happy state, Charlotte chatted with Eleanor beside the kitchen stove then floated upstairs, convinced she'd

239

never get to sleep after such an exciting day. Her godmother had placed a stone hot water bottle inside Charlotte's bed with her nightgown wrapped around it so she quickly settled into the warmth and knew nothing until past eight o'clock next morning when Eleanor knocked at her door, bringing her a cup of tea.

'I can't believe I slept so long.'

'You must have needed it. George called round for the key to open up and I've left some porridge in the warming oven. I'm off to work now. Enjoy your day, Charlotte. It's not a bad morning — cold but bright.'

Charlotte sat up in bed and sipped her tea. This was such a luxury. She looked down at her left hand. It would seem strange to be wearing a ring on her finger but wonderful to be doing so. She'd be very careful not to wear it for work. The idea of it being covered in oil or in contact with petrol made her shudder.

When Robert knocked at the back

door, she hurried to let him in. 'You're wearing your civvies,' she exclaimed. 'Does it feel strange?'

'It does rather,' he said, kissing her cheek. 'Mum insisted on washing every item of clothing she could lay her hands on. She reckons she'll have it all dry and pressed by tomorrow night. Now, are you ready for off?'

Charlotte didn't want to think of him leaving again, so swallowed the question she'd been about to ask as she reached for her big coat. Robert helped her into it.

'I have to return to base by Monday evening,' he said, sounding almost casual.

'Christmas is so close,' she said. 'It's a pity they couldn't have pushed your leave forward.'

He didn't comment as they left through the back door and locked it. He'd parked the Vauxhall outside her house.

'Let's say hello to your dad,' she said. 'Then we can walk down town and you

241

can tell me what you need to tell me. I think I can guess what it is.'

She linked her arm in his and ignoring the family's private entrance to the garage, they walked around the frontage, Charlotte eyeing the window display critically on the way. Any dust or dead insects and Jack would be instructed to remove them.

George was serving a customer but as soon as he'd finished, he called to them. 'Haven't you gone yet? If you don't look out, I'll find you both a job.'

Charlotte grinned. 'Just came to say Good Morning. This son of yours hasn't told me where his next posting's to be but I bet you know.'

'I didn't want to put a damper on your day, love,' said Robert. 'I only got home yesterday.'

'I know,' she said. 'I also know, if I'm a soldier's fiancée, I have to learn to cope with whatever's thrown at me. You're the one jumping in at the deep end. I imagine you're being sent to France. Am I right?'

Robert nodded. 'I'll be over there by Christmas.'

His father cleared his throat. 'Charlie, Postman delivered a card for you. It's in the office.'

'From Don?'

'I didn't look.'

Charlotte looked at her fiancé. 'I'll collect it then we'll go. Please don't look so worried. Nothing's going to spoil our day. I shan't let it.'

★ ★ ★

'I'm glad Don's got Christmas leave,' said Robert as they walked arm in arm towards the high street.

'So am I. I wonder where he'll be off to afterwards. I suppose it's right not to give details when you're writing to someone.'

'Security's a serious matter,' said Robert.

Charlotte gave his arm a squeeze. 'I hope he manages to write a decent letter to Pearl.'

'Has she not said he's been in touch?'

'I haven't seen her since she started her new job. She works long hours and she sleeps at the base. Any spare time, she needs to get home.'

'I expect you'd like to tell her our news. Maybe drop her a line in case she comes home and her ma and pa already know.'

'Gosh,' said Charlotte. 'I hadn't thought of that. Eleanor will be telling all her customers. Your dad will be telling all of ours.'

'They'll all be saying, wartime romance! These young folks are always in so much of a hurry!'

'Huh. I don't care what anyone says. I know better.'

'I've known for a very long time you and I would end up married one day.'

She stopped. 'Robert Costello! You are such a dark horse. I spent ages thinking you wouldn't give me a second glance.'

'I didn't want to be accused of cradle snatching.' He quickened his pace, putting his arm round her waist. 'Come on! Let's get this ring on your finger.'

'You young folks are always in a hurry,' she teased.

But he didn't relax his grip and when they arrived at the jeweller's, Charlotte's breath steamed up the windowpane as she gazed at the sparkling gems and shiny precious metals displayed upon black velvet.

'Robert,' she whispered after awhile. 'Look at the price of these — you mustn't even think of paying out so much money.'

He didn't answer.

'I really don't need diamonds. They're not my style. If they were, I'm sure Dad would let us have Mum's engagement ring. Let's go to Woolworths.'

'Charlotte, don't be daft. I'm not going to force you to have a diamond ring, whether it's your mother's or a new one, but you're going to have something a bit up together so you'd better make up your mind to do as you're told.'

'Well, can we go and look in the other jeweller's window then? I'd like something a bit different and I truly don't mind if it's second hand.'

'I give up. All right then, let's go and look. But no Woollies ring for my fiancée. Is that clear?'

'Yes, but I never knew you could be so bossy.'

He grinned and took hold of her hand. 'Some things are important and you're one of them.'

★ ★ ★

Charlotte insisted upon calling at Eleanor's Hair Salon to show off her ring.

'But you'll see her at teatime. Won't that do?' Robert looked puzzled.

'Just a quick pop in. She'll be busy but I'd like her to be the first person besides you to see me wearing my lovely ring.' Charlotte held out her finger so the wintry sunlight made the tiny seed pearls look extra lustrous.

'I'll stay outside,' said Robert, planting his feet firmly apart.

His new fiancée grinned. 'You look terrified. I promise I'll only be moments. Then maybe we could get the bus over to the prom and call in on your mother?'

She watched his face light up. 'Ma would love that.'

'Then that's what we'll do,' said Charlotte, pushing open the salon door.

Eleanor was at the desk, booking an appointment for a customer. Charlotte stood patiently until she'd finished then stepped forward and held out her left hand.

'Oh, love, it's beautiful. It suits you, it really does. Where did you get it?'

'Woollies! Only joking, Auntie El. It's an antique ring we spotted in that little place round the corner from Pinkham's. Honestly, the prices in there were outrageous. I've never been one to press my nose against a jeweller's window so I got quite a shock.'

Eleanor laughed. 'I can imagine. Where's the lucky man?'

'Lurking outside and I must go. We're off to show his mother now. Is it all right if Robert has tea with us this evening?'

'Of course it is. I've got something planned. Now off you go and enjoy the rest of your day.'

Charlotte joined Robert as he was consulting his wristwatch.

'There, I wasn't long, was I? Now for your mum.'

'We could pick up some bread rolls and a bit of ham down the road and eat them with her if you like.'

'Good job I've brought my ration book! Afterwards we could take Smuggler for a walk around the headland. What do you think?'

'I think Smuggler would be overjoyed. We won't walk too far though. I want to take you dancing tonight.'

She stopped walking. 'Dancing? Are you sure?'

He laughed. 'Are you afraid I'll tread on your toes?'

'No, I'm afraid I might tread on yours. I haven't been dancing for ages.'

He gently drew her towards the baker's. 'Nor have I. We can make mistakes together but I want us to have fun.'

'I am having fun.'

'Good,' he said.

★   ★   ★

'What did your mother think of Charlotte's ring, Robert?'

The happy couple were sharing a meal with Eleanor.

'She seemed very taken with it.'

'I'm not surprised,' said Eleanor. 'It's very delicate though. You'll need to take care of those seed pearls, Charlotte.'

'Don't worry, Auntie El, it'll be on a chain round my neck while I'm at work.'

Robert's face glowed. 'I shall think of you wearing it when I'm charging through the French countryside.'

There was a pause, each of them

doubtless considering the implications of the remark.

'But tonight you'll be steering me round the dance floor,' said Charlotte.

'Quite right too,' said her godmother. 'Saturday nights are meant to be spent having fun when a chap's home on leave.'

'That's what I told her,' said Robert. 'You could always come with us, Mrs Bennett.'

Eleanor smiled. 'Oh I don't think so, Robert, thank you. I shall curl up by the stove and listen to the radio while I write a letter. Should I mention your ring to Raymond, Charlotte? You might prefer to tell your dad yourself.'

'I'm happy for you to tell him. Give him my love and say I'll meet him at the station if he rings up to let me know the time.'

'How's the petrol situation?' Robert offered the bread plate to the other two then snaffled the remaining slice.

'I'm being very careful. Apart from special occasions like trips to the railway station and with a certain person being on leave, I try to walk everywhere. We're still getting grocery deliveries and the butcher's boy brings meat twice a week.'

'That'll stop next year,' said Eleanor. 'Apple pie for pudding?'

Charlotte groaned. 'I can't resist but how am I going to get round the dance floor?'

'You'll be like Ginger Rogers floating round in my arms,' said Robert. He jumped up to clear the used plates.

Eleanor bent her head towards her goddaughter. 'You've got a good 'un there. He's a lovely boy.'

'I know,' said Charlotte. If only he didn't have to go away from me, was the thought unspoken.

⋆　⋆　⋆

Charlotte hadn't been to Randalls since Pearl's parents invited her to join them at a tea dance on the day her friend became sixteen years of age. On that

251

occasion she'd been petrified at the thought of being asked to take to the floor yet equally petrified at the thought of becoming a wallflower. As it happens, she and Pearl must have looked younger than their real ages, dressed as they were in white socks and simple cotton dresses, so didn't face the problem of beating off prospective partners. They each had a dance with Pearl's father then circled the floor with one another, enjoying the chance to gaze round the sumptuous ballroom, a palace of dreams to two girls poised on the brink of womanhood.

'One day, we'll come here with our two handsome young escorts,' Pearl had said, gazing up at the balcony, supported by ornate scrolled columns, its rich cream paintwork decorated with gold leaf. 'We'll drink cocktails spiked with cherries on sticks and blow the expense.'

Charlotte had been concentrating on moving her feet where Pearl led. 'I suppose we'll wear silk stockings and shoes with straps and high heels.'

'Turquoise satin to match my gown,' Pearl had responded dreamily.

Dancing in Robert's arms that afternoon, Charlotte wasn't dressed like a fashion plate but wore a simple navy blue wool dress. Eleanor had tamed her goddaughter's blonde curls by styling them into a velvet snood. The white socks and girlish sandals were missing of course, replaced by silk stockings and navy blue suede shoes with little heels and crossover straps. The floor was crowded and for one moment, Charlotte could have sworn she caught a glimpse of Pearl in the arms of a tall young man. Maybe she'd conjured her friend up, reminiscing as she had been about that earlier occasion.

'Enjoying yourself?' Robert's mouth was close to her ear.

The band was playing a waltz and so far Charlotte thought she and Robert were acquitting themselves fairly well.

'I'm having a lovely time,' she said.

'What's this tune?' he asked

'Falling in Love with Love.'

He held her a little tighter. They hovered on the edge of the crowd of dancers. Robert seemed to prefer not taking them into the midst of the action, though Charlotte wondered if it might be safer to be hidden from the onlookers' eyes. He distracted her when he began crooning in caramel tones.

She pulled back from him in disbelief. 'You've got a really lovely voice, even if you don't know the words.'

He chuckled, drawing her closer once more. 'Did I not tell you I used to be a choir boy?'

Seamlessly he moved her on, following the flow of the dance. Suddenly a gap emerged between two waltzing couples, allowing her sight of a nearby table. A pair of brown eyes beneath a familiar cap of sharply styled auburn hair met hers. The owner of the pair of eyes sat alone at a table. Charlotte promptly pulled against the tide, disrupting the rhythm of the dance.

'Hey, the man's supposed to lead,' said Robert, jerking back to stare at her.

'I know. Just steer us to the right a bit and you'll find out why we need to stop dancing.'

'But I was enjoying it,' he protested. 'We're getting the hang of it now.'

Charlotte disengaged herself from his embrace, clutched his hand and dragged him after her. They pulled up at a nearby table.

'Pearl,' she said. 'Fancy seeing you here.'

'Charlie! I couldn't believe it when I caught sight of you.'

'I wonder why that would be. Mind if we join you?'

'Um . . . of course not,' said Pearl, her cheeks rivalling the bright pink of her dress. 'Hello, Robert.'

'Good to see you, Pearl.' He pulled out a chair for Charlotte and took his seat too.

'No turquoise satin?' Charlotte couldn't resist the dig.

'What do you mean?' Pearl frowned.

'Can I get you two ladies a drink?' Robert asked.

'I, um, my partner's fetching one for me.' Pearl's cheeks were beyond pink now.

'And he would be?' Charlotte's voice was cool.

'Philip McGirr. You remember the flying circus?' Pearl didn't wait for an answer. 'Phil's been posted to RAF Kimberley.'

'Phil the Pilot? Oh, Pearl, how could you?'

Robert rose. 'I'll go and find him while you two say what you have to say to each other. We should all have a drink together, Pearl. Charlotte and I are here to celebrate. I'm not sure what you're up to but please don't spoil my fiancée's evening. Or mine, for that matter!'

He made his way through the tables towards the bar.

Pearl turned to her friend. 'You two have got engaged?'

'Yes,' said Charlotte. 'I planned to

256

call round your house and tell your mum and dad. It's all happened in a hurry.'

'It's called war,' said Pearl. Her tone was bleak. 'That's why I'm here with Philip and not with Don. Please believe me, Charlie. Don's got Christmas leave and I can't wait to see him. Tonight's just a night out. I don't mean, anything bad by it. It's long hours and hard work in the NAAFI and the chance to put on a pretty dress and some lipstick was too much to resist.'

Charlotte bit her lip. 'Couldn't you have waited a few days longer? I'm not sure I trust you, Pearl.'

'Please don't look at me like that. Let me see your ring.'

Charlotte held out her left hand. Could not resist smiling with pure joy.

'Oh, it's so pretty, Charlie. Am I supposed to congratulate you or is that not etiquette?'

'Don't change the subject. Do you and my brother have an understanding or not?'

'We do. We really do.' Pearl leaned forward. 'I know as well as you do how much of a flirt Phil is. Surely you remember that's really how Don and I got together when the three of us came to the dance here?'

Charlotte nodded slowly. 'He met up with a girl from Coynesbury and you and Don were jitterbugging.'

'Yes. We went for a walk afterwards. Phil's still seeing that girl. They've been writing to one another but she's a nurse and they don't often get time off together.'

'Well, I hope she's an understanding sort of person.'

'The two most beautiful girls at the ball!' Philip the Pilot, looking debonair in his air force blue uniform, balanced a tray of drinks, elbow bent professionally as he arrived at the table.

'Hello, Philip,' said Charlotte. 'Fancy you being posted to Kimberley.'

'Quite a coincidence, ay?' He placed glasses before Charlotte and Pearl. 'One gin fizz and one — ta da — Pink Lady for the lady in pink!'

Pearl beamed. 'Thank you. I've just been explaining to Charlie how we're two lost souls, keeping each other company while our loved ones are elsewhere.'

Phil handed Robert his drink and the men took their seats.

'Your friend's entirely safe in my hands, Charlie. I've already explained the score to Robert so you can relax and enjoy yourselves.' The pilot raised his glass. 'Here's to the happy couple.'

Pearl echoed his words.

Robert squeezed Charlotte's hand beneath the table. 'Thank you,' he said. 'How about a toast to absent friends and loved ones?'

'Definitely,' said Charlotte. 'Maybe we should make a pact to meet here after peace is restored. All six of us,' she added, glancing at Pearl.

'Terrific idea,' said Philip. 'May I borrow Charlie for a dance, Robert? If she'll allow it of course.'

Robert looked slightly worried but

said, 'Have a dance, lovey. Phil's probably more expert than me.'

The couple took to the floor, leaving Pearl and Robert together.

'Um, would you like to . . . '

Pearl smiled. 'You don't have to dance with me, Robert. I'm happy sitting here. And very happy you and Charlie are engaged. Don will be really pleased for you, you know.'

'Thank you.' Robert fidgeted with his glass. 'Look, Pearl, you won't play around with Don will you? He's big enough and ugly enough to look after himself but I wouldn't want you to hurt him.'

'Goodness,' she said. 'I've no intention of hurting him.' She leaned across the table. 'Surely Phil's made it clear he and I aren't courting. I was serving breakfasts the other morning and he suddenly appeared with his tray. I'd already put sausages, egg and bacon on his plate before we looked each other in the eye. You can imagine how surprised I was.'

Robert nodded. 'Wartime can throw people together as well as drive them apart,' he said.

'There's such a thing as trust,' said Pearl quietly. 'I'll be true to Don. But if there's a bit of harmless fun to be had like this tea dance with friends, I'm not going to turn down the chance. Nor do I expect him to.' She twirled the cocktail cherry around in her Pink Lady.

Robert smiled. 'Funny how different we all are. When Don's home, I can't expect Charlotte not to go out with you and him if that's what you all want to do. But I hate the thought of other fellows dancing with her.'

'Other fellows as in Philip? He's the one who's based nearby.'

'He's the one she had a bit of a crush on. I know that for a fact.' Robert's face was pensive.

'Rubbish! You're being silly. You should know what she's like about speed. Charlie's the last person in the world to be a flighty piece. You just keep yourself safe and sound when you're off doing your despatch riding or whatever it is you do. Come back to her in one piece. That's an order.'

'One I'll happily obey — if that's what's meant to be.'

They stared at one another. Neither said a word and suddenly the other two were at the table.

'Why so serious?' Philip guided Charlotte back to her chair.

'Um,' said Robert. 'We were just trying to remember the name of a film star . . . I expect Pearl would like a dance now.'

Philip held out his hand. 'How's your foxtrot?'

Pearl giggled and got up. 'Only one way to find out.'

Left alone, Robert reached for Charlotte's hand. 'Nothing to worry about, I fancy.'

'Pearl and Don? It would seem not. To be fair, she's never been a racy kind of girl. It's just she seems to have altered her philosophy on life over the last months.'

'That's not surprising, is it? None of us can say with certainty how things will work out. All we can do is hope for the best.'

Charlotte smiled at him. 'Come on, let's try our hand at this. We should get our money's worth.'

'It's not my hands I have a problem with,' he said. 'Come on then. Let's go and shake a leg.'

Goodbye Till We Meet Again

It was hard to say goodbye to Robert, especially with Christmas so near. Charlotte summoned up all her resilience as she stood on the platform with him at Coynesbury Junction, awaiting his train.

'Your leave seems to have gone by in a flash,' she said.

'We packed a lot in.' He smiled down at her.

He looks so handsome, so very young, she thought as Robert reached for her left hand and gently removed her glove. 'Just one more look at you wearing my ring,' he said.

She felt the tears well up and had to bite her lip. 'You know I'll keep it close to me, even when it's not on my finger because I'm working.'

'You won't forget to send me a photograph?' Gently he pushed her glove back into position.

'Of course not. As soon as they're back from the chemist's I'll put one in the post. Might even write you a letter too.'

'Charlotte . . . I . . . '

'There's your train,' she said. 'Oh, you did pick up that pack of sandwiches your mum made you?'

'I did. Charlotte, there's so much I want to say but . . . you do know how much I care for you, don't you?'

She closed her eyes and buried her face in his shoulder, breathing in his essence. He put his arms around her and they stood quietly while the big steam engine huffed its way towards them. She knew this was not the moment for words. The closeness they'd achieved summed up the situation and like countless other couples, they faced separation and yearned for fate to look kindly upon them.

Charlotte broke away from her

fiancé's arms with reluctance. The moment had arrived. Robert took both her hands in his and mouthed 'good-bye' before planting one quick kiss on her mouth. He hoisted his kitbag over one shoulder and pulled open the door to the nearest compartment.

'See you soon,' he said. 'Drive back safely, my darling. I'll write as soon as I can. This isn't really goodbye. You and I are meant to be together.'

He stepped on board and she saw him lift his kitbag onto the luggage rack. She'd bought him a newspaper at the kiosk and she saw him clutching it as he mouthed *I love you* to her before squeezing into a vacant seat at the far side of the compartment.

Charlotte couldn't make her feet move from the spot. The train slid slowly away, getting up steam again, leaving her biting back the tears and waving even though she knew Robert could no longer see her.

★ ★ ★

'It's good to be home,' said Don, pulling off his boots and wriggling his toes.

'You won't hear any arguments from me,' said his dad, fingers laced around a cup of tea.

Charlotte, poured tea for herself and her brother and carried the cups to the table. 'Maybe you'd like yours by the stove, Don?'

'If no one minds. That train compartment was flippin' freezing.'

'Mine wasn't too bad,' said Mr Moore. 'I was worrying about your sister having to drive through fog. It looked pretty bad in some places.'

'Well, we're home now. Sorry I couldn't meet you at Coynesbury, Don. Both of you arriving on the same day . . . typical!'

'I was happy enough to get the bus,' said Don. 'Had a quick word with Robert's dad on my way round. He seemed to be coughing a bit.'

'I know,' said Charlotte. 'I've told him not to come in till it's better. The last thing he needs is to be breathing freezing fog. I'm sure we'll manage. Jack's got energy enough for three people.'

'I can take a turn on the pumps,' said her father. 'It'll be good to see my customers again.'

'We've tried to look after them all,' said Charlotte. 'You're here on leave though, Dad. And Don of course.'

Don took a swallow of tea. 'I'm quite happy to give you a break, sis. What's the plan for Christmas Day?'

'Eleanor's going to cook the turkey. Mr Graham got us one from his farmer friend as usual and I made a pudding back in November.'

'No, I meant, what time do we close the garage?'

Both her menfolk gazed at Charlotte. She swallowed hard.

'We've been closing at four these dark evenings. I see no reason to change it. People are used to the winter hours now.'

'That's my girl,' said her dad. 'If I

know Jack, he'll be anxious to earn what he can so he can do the full day but we'll let him scoot home for his dinner whatever time his mum tells him.'

'If I do the morning,' said Charlotte, 'you two can pay some calls and we'll have a bowl of soup to keep us going till the big dinner. Is that all right?'

'Perfect,' said Don. 'I'm meeting Pearl at the base tomorrow morning.' He hesitated. 'Is it all right if I use the Vauxhall? Will you need it, Dad?'

'You take it, son. I can walk to where I want to be. Is Eleanor here tonight or staying at her place?'

'She said she'd stay at the flat and do some catching up. She knows she's welcome, if she changes her mind.'

'I might stroll round later,' said Mr Moore. 'Make a couple of duty calls tomorrow on the cousins and so forth.'

'I need to call on Robert's parents at some point,' said Charlotte. 'I've got gifts from us both for them. We bought them while he was home on leave.'

'You can check up on George's cough then, love,' said her dad. 'Tell him I'll call round to see him Boxing Day morning if that's convenient.'

Slipping into the various gears, so easily, thought Charlotte. Getting on with the different layers of our lives even though Dad's sitting there in his khaki uniform as though he's never worn anything else. The same goes for Don. A few days ago it was Robert. Now I've no idea when he and I'll see one another again. Don hasn't said where his next posting is either. It's as though they want to keep their army life in a little box and not open it again until they have to.

The menfolk's rumble of laughter as they talked about a game of football interrupted Charlotte's musing. She smiled at them both. 'I thought we'd cheat and have a fish and chip supper tonight,' she said. 'Bags I Don goes to fetch them.'

★ ★ ★

Charlotte received a telephone call on Christmas morning. She heard the telephone ringing as she handed a customer his change. He was anxious to drive his family to visit relatives in Coynesbury and told her he wouldn't be surprised if they'd all be kipping on the sitting room floor that night, should there be too generous a snowfall.

She wished him luck and dashed towards the office, narrowly avoiding a fall as her foot skidded on an icy patch. 'Jack, get some salt down here, please!' Charlotte yelled the instruction and grabbed the telephone receiver, waiting impatiently while the operator went through her procedures.

'Hello?' Charlotte's voice was impatient. She hoped one of the regular customers hadn't run out of petrol and needed her assistance. It wouldn't be the first time.

'It's me,' said the voice.

'Robert! How marvellous to hear you. I bet there's a queue behind you.'

'Never mind that. How are you?'

'We're all fine. Hoping we don't get more snow.'

'Listen, Charlotte, I rang to wish you a Merry Christmas. I'm being sent to my next posting tomorrow. You may not hear anything for a while but I don't want you to worry. Promise?'

'That's easy to say, not so easy to do.'

'I got your letter and the photo. It's in my breast pocket. Enjoy your day, darling. I'll write when I can. Remember what I said.'

'Merry Christmas, sweetheart. I love you.' Suddenly the line went dead and Charlotte was left staring at the receiver. Moments earlier the voice she wanted to hear most in the world had drifted from the mouthpiece. Had he even heard her last words? The brief greeting had been like a tempting plate of food, whipped away after one or two delicious mouthfuls.

'No point in grumbling,' she whispered to herself.

Jack, scattering salt scraped from a big chunk purchased as soon as the

272

hard frosts set in, whistled a Christmas carol as he worked.

'Happy Christmas, darling Robert,' Charlotte called out loud. Then she began to sing in tune with Jack's whistling. *God rest ye merry gentlemen, let nothing ye dismay . . .*

Her father appeared, carrying a bulging shopping bag and walking gingerly along the cleared pathway down the pavement, Eleanor, wearing a fur coat and clinging to his arm. Picking up the sound of the carol, they began singing too, Raymond's mellow baritone and Eleanor's clear soprano tones mingling with Charlotte's husky voice and Jack's crystal clear piping. The four of them stood, paying homage to the spirit of Christmas, their breath rising like smoke on the frosty air.

' . . . tidings of comfort and joy . . . ' Probably not yet awhile, thought Charlotte. Meanwhile she had almost all her loved ones around her at this festive time. That was much more than many people could say.

'I'll come and relieve you as soon as I've had a hot drink and changed into my overalls,' said her dad. 'I'll fetch you a cuppa and a warm mince pie, Jack.'

When Charlotte left the garage forecourt, her dad, buttoned into his long foreman's coat and wearing a woolly balaclava, already had his head under someone's bonnet. She smiled to herself at the sight. It seemed an odd way to spend his precious leave but he looked happy enough. His business was literally his second home.

In the kitchen, Eleanor was putting the turkey into the oven. She wore a smart chocolate brown wool dress under a frilled, floral pinafore.

Charlotte stamped her boots on the mat inside the door. 'I had a phone call from Robert.' She struggled out of her big jacket. 'All these layers . . . lovely and warm in here though.'

'The bird's in the cooker and the old stove's nice and hot. I've put the pudding in the bottom oven, standing in a dish of hot water.'

'We shall have a feast,' said Charlotte. She ran to give Eleanor a hug. 'Guess who rang?'

'So how is your young man? What news?'

'They're moving him on tomorrow. He didn't say where and it may be a while before I hear from him.'

'He's marking your card. Making sure you know he won't be able to keep in touch, as he wants to. He's looking out for you, love.'

Charlotte sighed. 'I know but I hate the thought of not knowing where he is. He'll be overseas, destination unknown.'

'Charlotte, let me give you a piece of advice.' Eleanor hung the tea towel on the rail of the stove and sat down. 'You've got a good man there. He doesn't want to be away from you but he's got no choice in the matter. It won't help either of you, if you mope.' She raised her hand. 'I'm sorry if I sound harsh but you know I'm right. And your dad and your brother, not to

275

mention me, will worry about you if you go around like a month of Sundays.' She looked heavenwards. 'Not that there's anything wrong with a Sunday.'

Charlotte chuckled. 'I'm sorry if I behaved like a spoilt brat.'

'You didn't. You're behaving like a woman in love.' She covered her goddaughter's hand with her own. 'Keep your pecker up. Keep your man in your head and in your heart. Now, let's switch on the wireless and prepare the vegetables.'

'Remembering my brother will put away twice as many as you and me together,' said Charlotte. But she managed a smile.

The afternoon was spent companionably. After the garage closed they nibbled at warm mince pies and opened their festive gifts, Charlotte playing Postman as usual. Eleanor had crocheted her a beautiful shawl in a rich shade of crimson wool spun fine as a cobweb.

'You suit bright colours,' her god-mother said.

'It's absolutely beautiful. I think I shall make it part of my trousseau.'

'I should wear it and enjoy it, love,' said her dad. 'If I know El, she'll have something else up her sleeve for your trousseau.'

They oohed and aahed over their gifts, simple but welcome tokens of affection. At last the cooks shooed the men away, instructing them to light the gas fire in the living room and to lay the table, not forgetting to spread the dark green chenille cloth kept specially for festive occasions. One of Eleanor's clients had given her a box of luxury crackers, frothy white crepe paper trimmed with silver and gold lace, perfect against the fir tree green background.

Don lit the scarlet candle in the gleaming brass holder his sister had put ready with its own miniature holly wreath, just as she entered the room, carrying a small dish of homemade redcurrant jelly and the Sunday best silver condiment holder.

'You've done a good job,' she said. 'Mum would be pleased with us.'

'Reckon she would,' said her brother. He hugged her to him. 'I haven't told you properly how pleased I am about you and Robert.'

She held out her ring for him to admire. 'Pearl told me you'd be pleased when we bumped into her at Randalls last Saturday.'

She could have bitten her tongue off.

But Don only nodded. 'She mentioned she'd gone there with Phil.' He hesitated. 'Pearl also said you were edgy about her being there with him. Well, I know he's a bit of a bar fly but I don't think there's any malice in the fellow. He knows how things are between Pearl and me. I trust him is what I'm trying to say.'

'I'm glad,' said Charlotte. 'He's good fun. I suppose I jumped to conclusions. I do miss Pearl's company but our social lives have gone out of the window.'

'She misses you too. Maybe you could get to the pictures together some time. Keep an eye on each other.'

'You cheeky monkey.' Charlotte mock-punched her brother. 'As if we needed such a thing.'

'Come on you two,' called Eleanor. 'Your dad's carving. This is the big moment.'

Charlotte screamed as Don scooped her up and carried her into the kitchen, plonking her down beside the table.

'You've lost weight,' he said. 'It must be love.'

And so it continued, chatter and laughter ebbing and flowing as they dished up and carried the hot food through to the other room. The only silent moments were caused by the hearty appetites of the four, not by lack of conversational topics.

'That was a tip top meal,' said Raymond at last, sitting back in his chair. 'Compliments to the cooks.'

'A good joint effort,' said Eleanor. 'Just like the rest of the day. You men split the garage duties with Charlotte and she and I handled the dinner.' She smiled at her goddaughter. 'Even remembered to switch on for King George's speech.'

'He did a good job,' said Don. 'He's an example to us all.'

'He's another one having to do his duty and not what he really wants to do,' said Mr Moore.

'I wonder if the war will still be on by the time next Christmas comes around,' said Charlotte.

Eleanor shot her a warning glance.

'It's all right, everyone. You don't have to answer that,' Charlotte said hastily.

'I couldn't if I tried, love,' said her father. 'Why don't we finish with a little drop of Port?'

Don rose to fetch the bottle from the living room sideboard. 'I promised to walk round to Pearl's later, if that's in order,' he said.

'Don't mind us,' said his sister. 'You could do with a pair of snow shoes.

Why not take a short cut over the field?
It's probably easier walking.'

'Not a bad idea. I'll try not to wake
the sheep.'

'Try not to break the black out,' said
his father. 'Even on Christmas Night we
need to keep our wits about us.'

'It's all right, Dad,' said Charlotte.
'Don can take the torch with the special
cover. It's seen Auntie El and I home a
few times.'

'Do you want to come round to
Pearl's with me, sis?'

'No thanks, Don. You don't need me
hanging round. Give her my love, won't
you?'

★　★　★

Despite the snowy conditions, both
Don and his father travelled back to
their bases by train. Jack brought his
old toboggan round on the day they
needed to get to Coynesbury Junction
and the three piled the men's luggage
on board and trudged to Peel Bay

Station, Charlotte needing to remain at the garage as George Costello was still unwell.

Mrs Costello was concerned about her husband and the bookkeeping was falling behind though Eleanor had said she'd do her best to help, used as she was to keeping her own records for the taxman. New Year's Eve occupied a very low profile, with the women worrying more about pipes freezing than piping in the New Year.

One day merged into the next, the only bright spot being the knowledge that, winter solstice passed, daylight hours would eventually increase. As the savage winter days lost their bite and the weather became very cold rather than bone chillingly icy, Charlotte received a card from Robert. She turned it over quickly and scanned the brief message.

Here I am at last to tell you we're over the water, I'll give you an address next time I write. Not exactly the Ritz but we make do.

All my love, Robert xxx

It wasn't much to go on but at least she knew he was on French soil and as soon as he got back in touch she'd write a proper letter to him. The image on the postcard was of a large chateau, its name meaning nothing to her. Later of course, she could get out the atlas and look up the name. It wasn't a very productive exercise but somehow she felt it would make her feel closer to Robert.

She waved the card at Eleanor who'd abandoned opening the salon on Mondays. 'Private Costello has communicated.'

'I told you it wouldn't be easy for him. Can you write back or is he of no fixed abode?'

'He says he'll let me know his address when he can. How strange it all is. Would he be sleeping in a tent?'

Eleanor pursed her lips. 'Soldiers sleep wherever they can. They might be in tents at first then as they push on towards the enemy lines, they could end up sleeping in hen houses, barns, under hedges or even in churchyards.'

Charlotte felt as if she was choking. 'In such cold weather, that could be very dangerous. It's just not fair on those poor soldiers!'

'War isn't fair, Charlie. There are countless German wives and sweethearts feeling just as you do now. A lot of their men were sent off last summer and are probably still out there. They weren't kitted out for cold weather. At least the boys going out like Don and Robert have embarked equipped for winter.'

Charlotte turned the card over again and traced her forefinger over Robert's signature bold, curly letter R. 'I know we all have to be patient. They're the ones fighting for us.'

'Meanwhile,' said her godmother, 'I'll take myself off to the high street and see what's about. When I come back, I'll make up a big pot of stew. There's a bit of meat left from yesterday to give it some extra zip.' She frowned. 'Have you left Jack on his own?'

'No. I forgot to say, George is back at work. He says his chest's much better now the extreme cold has gone.'

'That's a relief. Does this mean Mrs Costello will be in later?'

'She will,' said Charlotte. 'I can show her Robert's card.'

'Kisses and all?' Eleanor teased.

'Kisses and all,' said Charlotte. 'What you said about the Germans has really touched me. The ordinary soldiers are all just boys, most of them, aren't they?'

★   ★   ★

A few mornings later, a small red sports car pulled up at the pumps while Charlotte spoke on the telephone to a customer. She watched through the window as Jack approached the driver, ready to serve him. But the motorist wriggled out of his seat and as he stretched to full height, Charlotte realised it was Philip McGirr, in his RAF uniform. He headed towards the office, leaving Jack to top up the tank.

Phil lounged in the doorway, his gaze fixed on Charlotte. She ignored him as she continued her conversation then replaced the receiver and raised her eyebrows.

'Good morning, beautiful,' he said. 'I hoped you'd be on duty.'

'Is that your car?' Charlotte peered through the window.

'Unfortunately not,' he said. 'It belongs to my Commanding Officer and he's given me the use of it for a few hours. I'm not on ops again until tomorrow.'

'Aren't you the lucky one? So where are you off to?'

'Where do you want me to take you?'

Charlotte chuckled. 'You're incorrigible, Phil. I should call your bluff and say let's drive down the coast and have lunch.'

'That's a terrific idea, Charlie. Off you go and powder your nose or whatever while I settle up with your

286

young mechanic. Nice lad, very polite by the way.'

'He's doing very well and I'm quite happy to take your money, thank you. Seriously, Philip, how can you plan to go joy riding with petrol supplies the way they are?'

He tapped the side of his nose. 'All sorted, my dear. Will you come with me? Seriously, I mean.'

'Seriously no, Phil. I can't abandon the garage on a whim. I'm surprised you haven't got Pearl in tow.'

He shook his head. 'I haven't seen her for a few days.'

'So you thought you'd go for second best?' But Charlotte was smiling.

The corners of his mouth drooped. 'Definitely not the case but I thought it was worth a try. How's that fiancé of yours getting on? Heard from him?'

'I have. He doesn't say much but I love getting Robert's letters and writing back of course.'

'I envy him.'

'Being an Army despatch rider? Surely not?'

'Having a beautiful fiancée to come home to,' said Phil, straightening his tie.

'You're such a flatterer. Maybe you should try concentrating on one girl-friend instead of a string of them.'

'Maybe I should.' He grinned at her. 'I might call round Pearl's house and see if she can come out to play.' He watched Charlotte's face. 'Oh dear, what have I said now?'

'You know perfectly well why I'm frowning. Pearl's spoken for.' Even as she said it, Charlotte remembered her friend's comment about not wanting to miss an opportunity for a bit of harmless fun.

'I know Pearl's your brother's girl-friend but I do like to spread a little sunshine wherever I can. I would've thought Don would be pleased I'm thinking of her welfare.'

'I give up. Are you still seeing the nurse?'

His face glowed. 'Yes. Little Nurse

Compton is a super girl but she seems to work all the shifts under the sun. I rang the nurses' home this morning.'

'Ah, so I'm actually your third choice!'

He reached across and gently chucked her under the chin. 'I'd better go before I put my foot in it even deeper.' He peered through the window, reaching for his wallet. 'Your lad's given me four gallons and it looks like he's putting the airline away now. I'll give him a little tip.'

'That's up to you, Phil but there's really no need.' Charlie took the bank note from the pilot and counted out his change.

'Least I can do. He's cleaned the windscreen as well.'

'All part of the service.'

'See you around, Charlie,' said Philip. 'Don't worry about your friend's reputation. I'm quite happy to take her ma out too, provided Pearl squashes into the back seat. Cheerio!'

Charlotte was still smiling when Jack

walked into the office.

'What did you think of the daredevil pilot, Jack? He used to be part of the flying circus before he joined the RAF.'

The lad shuffled his feet. 'He's a friendly sort of bloke, for a Brylcreem boy. He gave me a nice tip but I'm a bit taken aback.'

'What's troubling you?' Charlotte couldn't think what had happened to make the young apprentice look so uneasy.

'I couldn't help noticing what he had on the back seat. It was when I was checking the tyres and the spare one, like George taught me.'

'Go on.' Charlotte held her breath.

'I saw a blooming big box of posh chocolates. I've never seen the like of it before but I didn't say a word.' Jack bit his lip. 'When he came out after talking to you, he asked me how things were at home.'

'What did you say?'

Jack shrugged. 'Something like, we manage 'cos my dad's got an allotment and he shoots the odd rabbit some-times.' Jack's cheeks reddened. 'He's not a poacher. Dad don't trespass on nobody's land.'

'Of course not,' Charlie soothed. 'Maybe those chocolates belong to Flight Officer McGirr's commanding officer.' She spread her hands. 'He's the one who owns the car, Jack. They might even have been bought before rationing began. We mustn't jump to conclusions.'

'I s'pose not.' Jack's voice was wistful. 'What wouldn't I give for a box like that to give my ma. Strawberry creams, cherries in brandy and Russian Caramels . . . flippin' heck.'

Charlie nodded. 'Mrs Bennett's got a sweet tooth. We make a good pair — she has my sugar ration and I have her butter coupons.'

'I s'pose the chocs would've had to have been bought before rationing began,' said Jack. 'You'd need all of our street to give up their coupons before you could buy a box like that.'

He turned back to the workshop leaving Charlotte to ponder why anyone would ride around with a luxury item openly displayed on the back seat of their car. Even if the chocolates were purchased legitimately, before the advent of rationing, it didn't set a very good example when most people were making do and wishing things could be different.

Maybe Phil planned to drop off the box at the nurses' home for his lucky young lady. With all her heart Charlotte hoped there wasn't something more sinister to worry about. After all, Philip could have been passing the time of day when he questioned Jack about his family's circumstances. It didn't mean he was checking whether the lad might be interested in purchasing black market goods.

She shivered. This war hadn't been going a year and already she was heartily sick of it.

Suspicion and Shock

The year progressed, letters and cards from Robert infrequent though cheerful. Sometimes Charlotte's eyes brimmed with tears as she tried to imagine the conditions under which he and his fellow-soldiers existed.

Always careful to conserve her petrol ration, somewhat better than the standard one, because of the work she performed, Charlotte drove Eleanor to Huddlesham where they collected Mr Moore, Sergeant Moore to be accurate, from the camp gates before driving into the town.

They found a good restaurant where they enjoyed a lunch that made Charlotte and her godmother exclaim over the portions. Mr Moore seemed well, listening enthusiastically when his daughter spoke about the garage and how good it was to see Robert's dad and mum enjoying their roles, not forgetting Jack of course.

When the lunchtime conversation turned to the political situation and the war's progress, Charlotte's father shook his head, the lines around his eyes and mouth deepening.

'We're in for a very tough time,' he said. 'Shock waves will affect us all. I'm relieved Peel Bay, though it's on the coast, isn't slap bang close to the air base.'

For a moment Charlotte wanted to mention Philip's box of chocolates but thought better of it. She had no proof of shady goings on and hadn't seen the pilot since. Pearl had mentioned seeing him at the base in the course of her duties but to Charlotte's relief, her friend seemed to want to speak more and more of Don, asking for snippets of information about him and proudly producing a pair of socks she'd knitted for her sweetheart.

Charlotte said as much to her father as he ate the last of his Bakewell tart.

'That's good to hear,' he said. 'It means a lot to a man fighting far from home to know he has a wife or sweetheart caring about him.'

Charlotte noticed Eleanor look down at her plate, rather than catch anyone's eye. She'd gone through this whole tragic business during the First World War of course. Even though Mr Moore wasn't on active service, he, like many other British citizens, was vulnerable to all kinds of unpleasant situations. Hopefully he'd be able to return home before too long, though knowing her dad, Charlotte suspected he wouldn't let the small matter of celebrating his fiftieth birthday soon deter him from what he considered his duty.

Charlotte looked at her watch. 'Thank goodness for the lighter evenings,' she said. 'We don't have to rush back. Do you two want to wander off somewhere? I'd like to look at a few clothes shops and I need to buy some airmail notepaper. My supply's a bit low.'

'Well, you mustn't run out, that's for sure,' said her father. 'Do you fancy a walk along the river, El? They say it's very pleasant.'

'So long as you're happy to go off on your own, Charlotte?'

'I'm quite happy alone, thanks. Shall we meet up for a cup of tea, two hours from now?'

'There's a teashop opposite the cathedral,' said Eleanor. 'It has a kettle painted on its signboard. I noticed it when we walked from the car.'

They gathered their belongings and Charlotte set off alone, pleased with her idea. Eleanor and her dad rarely had time to themselves and since she and Robert began courting, she realised how precious those moments in one another's company were.

Besides, she wanted to visit the cathedral, not only to admire the architecture and beautiful stained glass but also to spend a few quiet moments in prayer. There was much she wanted to say and she hoped the ancient sacred atmosphere would have a calming, healing effect.

The huge grey stone building loomed ahead but Charlotte decided to explore the shops first. Then she could linger in the cathedral for the remainder of the time. There were several drapers and ladies' outfitters dotted around the town centre and she browsed these until she spotted a stationer's and went in to buy her stationery.

As she walked up the flagstone path leading to the cathedral's main door, she wondered how many others had preceded her. The labour invested in these holy buildings always made her feel overawed by the levels of determination and commitment. In that way, it was rather like the war effort, she supposed.

Wandering along the main aisle her gaze focused upon the largest of several impressive stained glass windows. The fruit gum colours of the panes glowed green, raspberry, amber and violet in the afternoon sunshine.

Charlotte walked on towards a secluded side chapel, descending the short flight of worn stone steps to sit quietly, meditating and asking the questions popping in and out of her head at such regular intervals.

Why does such evil exist in this world of ours? How can we bring this ugly war to an end? How can we keep peace for the future?

Finally, when will Robert come home to me? She knew it was a selfish thing to ask but somehow couldn't help herself. She knew he'd no control over his own destiny but she prayed with all the strength of her pent up longing for his safe return and also for that of her brother.

There remained a few minutes before she was due to meet her father and godmother. Charlotte picked up her tan leather shoulder bag and rose from the pew. She gave a special smile to the statue of a female saint who seemed to be looking straight at her, before returning to the main area. A few

298

sightseers lingered, also people seated in the pews, lost in prayer or simply relishing the peaceful atmosphere. It was hard to imagine the dark scenes taking place all those miles away, the clatter of artillery, the yells of the men, the rumble of heavy vehicles on the move. Here she was experiencing England at its best. It was dreadful to think of such tranquillity being threatened.

Out in the sunshine she squinted against the brightness, almost mowing down a young man in uniform.

'I'm so sorry,' she gasped. 'It was my . . . Phil! What are you doing here?'

Stunned, Charlotte hitched her bag back on her shoulder and shaded her eyes to look up at Philip the Pilot.

'Charlie, old girl, what an amazing surprise! What the devil are you doing here?'

'I asked you first,' she reminded him.

'So you did. Well, I have a pal flying Spitfires out of Dales Cross.' He scratched his chin. 'Of course, I remember now. Your father's at the training camp near here, isn't he?'

Charlotte eyed Philip with interest. He looked distinctly uncomfortable as he put down the small suitcase he'd been carrying.

'Eleanor and I drove up today,' she said. 'I'm meeting her and Dad of course, just across the way. Would you like to join us? You're very welcome.'

A spasm of what she could only describe as panic crossed his face. 'Oh, my dear, you're very kind but I have an appointment.'

'At the cathedral? Don't tell me you're marrying the nurse.' Charlotte couldn't resist the jibe.

Phil's laugh sounded a little forced. 'Um . . . well, I have to meet someone at the hotel just up the road. I'm rather early so I thought I'd go inside here and sit quietly for a while. You know how it is.'

'Quite. Well, I'd better go and join the others.' She caught hold of his arm. 'You will take care, Phil, won't you?

There are some very strange folk around.'

'You sound just like my dear mama,' he said, leaning to kiss her cheek. 'I'm looking out for myself, Charlie, I really am. I'll, er, try and call at the garage soon.' But he didn't meet her eyes.

She watched his retreating back. Something was going on. Why wouldn't he go into the hotel to wait? He loved cocktail bars and chatting to all and sundry. Why the sudden interest in a religious building? It didn't sit right but she didn't have time to shadow him and if she said anything to her father, he'd doubtless advise her to keep her nose out of the pilot's business.

If Phil McGirr should be up to no good, she'd be better off distancing herself. The words rang clear in her head as if her dad had already said them. Charlotte squared her shoulders. She'd say nothing about her fears but as soon as she could, she'd talk to Pearl and see if she had any ideas on the subject. Black marketeers trod a precarious tightrope but plenty of them, like the smugglers she'd read about during schooldays, were prepared to take the risk. If only she could have peeped inside that small brown suitcase.

* * *

The day after the Huddlesham trip, Charlotte decided to call on Pearl's mother. She learnt Pearl's next visit was expected two days later so she left the brief note she'd written ready for her friend to open when she turned up.

In due course, Pearl, dressed in a mint green costume and cream blouse, arrived at the Corner Garage just as Charlotte was about to do her banking.

'Come with me,' Charlotte begged. 'I can't delay the banking but I really need to ask you something.'

'All right,' her friend agreed. 'As long as I can get home again for tea with Mum at five.'

Charlotte always took her paying in book, little wads of bank notes and moneybags, bundled up like fish and chips in newspaper, inside a wicker shopping basket.

'You look like Red Riding Hood,' teased Pearl as they walked along.

'It's the Wolf I'm more interested in.'

'What wolf?' Pearl glanced sideways at Charlotte. 'Are we speaking in code now?'

'No, but we must be careful not to be overheard. I'm concerned about a mutual friend. His initials are P. M.'

Pearl's pace slowed. 'Peter Martin? The butcher's son who had his eye on you a few years ago?'

'Gosh, Pearl, I'd forgotten about Big Pete. No, think flying circus.'

'Ah. I get it. What about him?'

'I have certain suspicions.' Charlotte explained Jack's surprise at seeing the enormous box of confectionery. She mentioned how the pilot asked Jack how his family were managing. Then she described her chance encounter outside Huddlesham Cathedral. Pearl listened but seemed unimpressed.

'Honestly, Charlie, Phil comes from a well-off family, you know. He might've been given the chocs and decided to pass them on to his ladylove. As for asking Jack how his family was doing — surely that was only being polite?'

'Odd that he'd hoped to take you or, as a last resort, me, out for a drive don't you think? Why would he risk being questioned over the chocolates?'

'I don't know. Maybe he planned to turn up at the hospital and ask for his little nurse.' Pearl made a tutting sound. 'You know what he's like — he could charm the starched cap off a ward sister in a twinkling.'

'I agree. Maybe we should give him the benefit of the doubt. But he seemed so shifty when we bumped into one another. He put his suitcase down and moved so his legs concealed it.'

'Charlie, I just don't know. I haven't been out with him since that night at Randalls. I knew deep down Don wouldn't like me keeping company with another fellow. I'm not stupid and I really am fond of that brother of yours.' She linked her arm in Charlotte's.

'What do you think I should do?'

'If you're worried that much and you think someone should talk to him, I could maybe have a word,' offered Pearl. 'But I don't always see him. My duties vary, you know. What about writing him a letter?'

'To say I suspect he's running a black market operation and he should stop immediately?'

'Or, if he doesn't bring you some nylon stockings soon, you'll spill the beans. I think not, Charlie. This needs diplomacy, in my humble opinion.'

'Pearl, please don't put yourself in difficulty just because of my suspicions.'

'You do sound worried, dearie. I'll do my best but I can't promise anything will come of it.'

'At least I'll feel I've tried.' Charlotte sighed. 'If he's only dabbling, he might decide not to get in any deeper.'

'This is getting more and more like a spy thriller,' said Pearl. 'Here we are. I'd better see you inside just in case we're being followed.'

They caught one another's eye and giggled. Just for a moment, Charlotte felt it was like back in the good old days, when gossiping and giggling in the company of her dearest friend formed a large part of her life. Pearl was trying to cheer her up but Charlotte hoped Phil wasn't walking on the dark side. Even though he wasn't a close friend, she cared about him in a sisterly way. Also, she hated to think of the implications if he should be guilty and faced retribution. If only Don or Robert was around. They'd soon discover what was happening.

* * *

After her chat with Pearl, Charlotte concentrated on the business and helped her godmother with the domestic chores as much as possible.

Extra daylight and warm weather helped enormously and sometimes, when Charlotte opened up the garage, often as early as 7.30 a.m., she wished she could stroll off towards the old harbour and along the promenade, taking advantage of the newly-minted air.

Some evenings, if they weren't too tired from being on their feet most of the day, Charlotte and Eleanor walked down to the prom. Both agreed it didn't seem right to see Fun Land with its stalls and rides battened down instead of dressed up in bright lights and belting out loud music.

Occasionally they'd call on Robert's parents and Charlotte would sometimes take Smuggler out, leaving Eleanor to chat. On one such occasion, Robert's father asked if he could walk with her.

'I don't like the sound of what's going on over there, Charlie,' he said, face sombre as they walked along the firm golden sands while Smuggler raced around, terrorising unsuspecting seagulls.

'Let's perch over there,' she suggested, pointing to a flat rock a few yards away.

'I'm not scaremongering,' he said once they settled. 'I try not to let the boy's mother dwell on the situation but I'm telling you, Charlie, I wish Robert wasn't over there.'

'Same here,' she said. 'But I imagine he's good at his job. He's got the motorcycling skills, he can do his own maintenance and he has a good sense of direction. The perfect despatch rider, and maybe there are worse jobs than the one he's doing.'

'You're right, I know,' said George. 'Things will take their course and there's nothing we can do about it.'

Charlotte watched Smuggler rush back from the shoreline as a wave broke into froth and bubbles almost drenching the little dog. 'It's almost a year since he joined up and months since his leave. No wonder you both miss him.'

'Having you in our lives has helped a lot,' he said. 'That's really what I wanted to say. If you get a letter you tell us how he's doing.'

'And you do the same for me,' she chimed in. 'But we don't truly know what he's doing, do we? Someone like me can only imagine what it's like. That's why I try not to think of him as being away at war. I like to picture him working at the fair or with me riding pillion through the town. It's escapism, I know.'

'Nobody's going to blame you for that, love. Least of all Robert, I imagine.' He picked up a stick and flung it for Smuggler to collect. 'We'd best get back but I've enjoyed our talk.'

'We don't do much of that at the garage, do we? I'm writing again tomorrow so I'll tell Robert we took Smuggler for a walk. Not that it's sparkling news.'

'Believe me, bits and pieces like that'll help keep him sane,' said George. 'Now look at that pesky puppy . . . Smuggler, put that down this minute!'

* * *

Robert's next communication must have crossed in the post with Charlotte's letter to him. She swooped upon the postman as soon as she saw him approaching the garage and was rewarded with another cheerful but brief message.

My dear Charlotte, this is to let you know my new address for mail. Please tell my parents. I'm on the move soon so please forgive my not writing a proper letter. If you get a chance to send some soap, it would be much appreciated.
Your ever-loving Robert xxx

Charlotte copied out the address, which gave no clue as to his whereabouts. She left it on the desk for Robert's mother to find when she came in later. Why couldn't he be granted some leave? Whatever his father argued about his son's suitability for the role

310

he'd been given, it didn't alter the fact he'd been away too long. Eleanor was right. Being patient played a very important part in the war effort, she decided.

As for her brother, nobody had heard anything for a long time but the retreat from the Dunkirk beaches brought speculation from his family as to his whereabouts. It was a great relief when Don rang from an army camp further east to say he'd been rescued and would be home on leave before long.

Peel Bay, like countless other English coastal towns, became involved in defence preparations. Emotions were whipped up as well as determination to take practical action.

Don didn't want to talk about what had happened and Charlotte didn't press him. He slept a lot and it was a relief when he began spending time in the garage, talking to George and Jack and of course, seeing Pearl whenever possible. Sometimes he'd cycle to the base so he could ride back with her when she finished her shift.

After Don rejoined his regiment, Charlotte tried to take each day as it came. Her impatience subsided and as autumn loomed she resigned herself to another long, hard winter but there were worse things to concern her than chilblains. At Christmas, she and Eleanor spent a quiet time together as none of the men was home on leave. The two women decided to buy war bonds instead of giving each other presents though Charlotte tried her hand at making bookmarks as gifts for female friends and relations, sticking on scraps of fabric from her godmother's sewing box. She surprised herself by enjoying this task.

'You see, your creative side is showing itself,' Eleanor told her, eyes twinkling at the sight of the first masterpiece.

'It's rather soothing, this kind of work,' said Charlotte.

Neither of them spoke of the continuing silence surrounding Robert's whereabouts. When the New Year was only five days old, George arrived for work, carrying a letter, his expression concerned though he managed a smile for Charlotte.

'I'm afraid there's some news,' he said, putting his hand up to silence her. 'Please don't jump to conclusions. Robert's all right but he's been injured and taken to hospital in Sicily.'

'How bad is it?' Charlotte clasped her hands in front of her mouth and gnawed on a knuckle.

Robert's dad held out the letter. 'All it says is he's been wounded in action, he's recovering and will be repatriated when he's fit to travel.'

Her heart sank. Much as she wanted to see him again, she couldn't bear the thought of Robert being in pain and suffering who knew what disability. She skimmed the handwritten letter, signed by an officer called James MacLean.

'His CO, I expect,' said George. 'At least we can write to the lad.'

Charlotte's eyes filled with tears. 'How I wish I could go out there to be

313

with him.' She handed the letter back.

Robert's dad cleared his throat. 'We can't do anything but hope for his full recovery.'

Charlotte nodded. She didn't want to examine the possibilities, not at that moment anyway.

★   ★   ★

She wrote as soon as she could. But she found it difficult to release on to the page the feelings welling up inside her, causing her to sniff a couple of times and angrily rub her eyes when a teardrop sneaked down one cheek. The letter she wrote to the young man occupying first place in her affections ended up sounding as if she was a friend looking forward to seeing him whenever he felt able to visit.

'Oh dear,' she sighed to herself. 'I can't send this, I really can't.'

The last words, spoken aloud, attracted the attention of Eleanor who sat in the comfortable old chair, knitting yet another pair of socks.

'Are you writing to Robert?'

'Yes.' Charlotte laid down her pen. 'The trouble is, I daren't say what I really want to say. It'll be too sentimental and I want him to recover quickly — not wallow in mawkish thoughts.'

'Hmm.' Eleanor thought for a moment. 'It sounds as if you're not writing from the heart then?'

'Of course I'm not, Auntie El. Didn't I just say that?'

'Why don't you begin again? It needn't be lengthy. Tell him what you really want him to know, not what you think is best.'

Charlotte stared at her. 'Let my emotions show, you mean? What if he decides I'm soft in the head?'

'Believe me, he won't. He'll have nurses and doctors being brisk and cheerful. He'll be doing his best to keep a stiff upper lip and he'll hate the thought of you worrying about him.'

Charlotte listened then began a

second letter, one she hoped, when Robert opened it in his narrow hospital cot in Sicily, would warm his heart, bring unashamed tears to his eyes and confirm what he already knew.

My darling Robert

Your CO wrote to your dad to let him know you were wounded. I can't tell you how sorry I am to hear this. My heart goes out to you and, although I don't know what your injuries are, I hope you'll heal fast and grow stronger each day. As soon as you do, they'll be able to send you on leave. We'll all be waiting for you with open arms — me most of all. I miss you very much, my darling. But your regiment will be missing you too, I'm sure of that. Knowing you, you've achieved lots.

Their loss will be our gain! All of us love you and want to help bring you back to full strength. So come home soon, my lovely, brave Robert.

All my love, Charlotte xxx

She put down her pen and read it through. Eleanor's advice had helped her voice her true feelings for her fiancé. Before she could change her mind, she folded the flimsy sheet and placed it in an envelope, sealed it and added the address.

Eleanor looked up from her knitting. 'Feel better now?'

'Much better. Thanks, Auntie El.'

'He'll come back to you. Don't ask me how I know, I just do.'

★ ★ ★

Sometimes Charlotte felt it was hard to recall life before the war began. Those first months after Mr Chamberlain's dreaded announcement hit the airwaves now seemed like a dress rehearsal for the real thing. Sleepy little Peel Bay hadn't suffered from the Blitz and somehow the airbase kept on operating.

Pearl dropped in on Charlotte a couple of months after the news of Robert's hospitalisation. They sat in the little office where Pearl had worked.

She gazed round her as if committing everything to memory. 'I've got something to tell you,' she said.

Charlotte steeled herself though she had a fair idea what was coming.

'I've volunteered to join the WAAFs.'

'I'm not surprised,' said Charlotte. 'I shall miss you, even if we haven't seen much of each other recently.'

'I'll miss you too, Charlie, and my folks of course.' Pearl shook her head sadly. 'Who knows when I'll see Don again? I feel I want to do something more significant than dishing up fried eggs and bacon to the pilots.'

'I understand. You must write to me and tell me how you're getting on. My list of pen pals is growing.' Her brow creased. 'I'd almost forgotten about Philip. Is he still around?'

'Did he not call to say goodbye? I felt sure he would. Last time I saw him, he was off up north on a posting. I heard through the grapevine he'd been given a warning — let's say about certain shady activities and leave it at that.'

'Let's hope he doesn't blot his copybook then. I wonder if anything will come of his friendship with Nurse Compton. I hope the chocolates reached her in the end.'

Pearl shrugged. 'I don't know what you're talking about.'

'It's not important. I think I embarrassed him that day we bumped into one another at Huddlesham. He's such an unlikely person to be visiting a cathedral.'

'Maybe he was asking for guidance?'

Charlotte smiled. 'You could be right. War does strange things to people.'

Pearl looked at her watch. 'I'll write as soon as I can.' She put her arms around her friend. 'Take good care of yourself, Charlie.'

Charlotte hugged her back. 'You too, Pearly Queen.'

'My goodness, you haven't called me that for years.'

'You always hated the nickname, that's why.'

Pearl's smile was wistful. 'Isn't it strange, the stupid things we used to complain about? Now look at us.'

Charlotte walked to the forecourt with her. 'I refuse to say goodbye,' she said. 'I'll pop in on your mum when I can.'

'Thanks, Charlie. She'll appreciate that. Let's say *Au Revoir* then.'

As her friend walked away, Charlotte wondered just when she'd see any of her loved ones again.

Laying Foundations

Life became even busier for Charlotte, giving her no cause to wonder why she remained in a backwater while most of the people she cared about were scattered around the world. A gun battery had been installed on a small island a mile from the coast and this meant more business for the garage. She delivered cans of fuel to several different outlets now as well as coping with her normal duties.

Jack arrived one morning with a slice of watermelon grin on his face. He asked if he could speak to her.

'You're volunteering.' She knew immediately.

He nodded. 'I'm eighteen next week and I've passed the medical. I went to the recruiting office in Coynesbury.'

Charlotte knew, as a volunteer, he could ask to join which branch of the

321

services he preferred. 'The Navy?'

'Yes.' His face shone with pride. 'I'll miss you all. I expect you'll need to take on another lad. It's too much for you and George on your own.'

'Don't worry about us. I wish you all the best. Now, better go and see what George needs you to do.' She watched him hurry off, her thoughts whirling.

As soon as she could, she wrote a short note to her father, asking him to telephone her. She dropped the letter into the nearest pillar-box before she went to lunch and crossed her fingers he'd approve of her suggestion.

Mr Moore rang next evening shortly before closing time.

'Jack's a good lad,' he said. 'And who am I to complain about someone volunteering? You'll need another youngster though.'

'But will we? I'm wondering how much longer you want to be away from home, Dad. It's time we started to think about the long term future of the business.'

'We none of us know how long the war's going to last,' said her father.

'No, but you've given much more than many other men your age. Why don't you come home? Take over the business again. I'm also thinking of Don's future.' And Robert's, she added silently.

She held her breath; her desire to keep her loved ones close to her, overwhelming her practical side. Robert would soon be pronounced fit enough to travel back to England. Who knew what condition he'd be in or whether he'd be fit enough to resume his military duties? Changing circumstances brought fresh problems and Charlotte was anxious for the family business to function efficiently.

'Do you want to follow in Pearl's footsteps, my girl?'

'If I wasn't engaged to Robert, I would,' she said. 'But I can't think of joining up, the way things are.'

The silence made her wonder if her father had been cut off. Then he spoke again.

'I've been thinking hard about my

future,' he said. 'My business means a lot to me and if my family needs me, I don't think I should hesitate about coming home.'

Charlotte's heart seemed to give a joyful back flip. 'You've absolutely no need to feel guilty,' she said. 'Anyway, knowing you, you'll be joining the Home Guard. There's another thing,' she said. 'I think Eleanor's finding things difficult. It's a lot for her, coming and going between her place and ours. She's trying to hold the salon together with just one junior.'

'Do you want to go and lend a hand there?' His voice rippled with mirth.

Charlotte chuckled. 'Poor clients! No, Dad, I'll do whatever's needed for the garage but if you're back, I can do something more for the war effort — there are ways I know I can help.'

'All right,' he said. 'I'll drop you a line as soon as things are sorted out this end. 'Tell El to keep her chin up.'

She put down the phone with an enormous sense of relief.

* * *

When the day came, she knew exactly what she would wear. He'd always admired her in her sapphire blue tweed suit. The afternoon was crisp and cool and she'd chosen a white blouse with a frilled front to wear beneath her jacket. The navy blue shoes with the little heel hadn't had an outing in a while and her godmother, bless her, produced a pair of nylon stockings she said she'd been saving for such an occasion.

Her father had swiftly settled back to his former routine. That morning he'd washed and polished his precious Vauxhall so the car gleamed in the sunshine as Charlotte opened the driver's door.

'Take as long as you want, love,' he said as she settled herself behind the wheel. 'Robert might need a rest after the train journey. You could have tea in that little hotel.'

'Thanks, Dad. It's exciting having

him come home but . . . well, it's been a long time.'

'He'll be returning with battle scars. Let him make the running.'

'I will.' She looked down at her engagement ring, remembering the day Robert proposed to her in the teashop. 'It's not too far to walk to the Corner House. I'll see how he feels.'

Charlotte started the engine and waved to her father before driving away. How many times had she made this trip to Coynesbury station over the last few years? Robert's last letter, written in a shaky hand, had warned her not to expect miracles. We'll need to talk, he'd said. Yes, of course they needed to talk but she had ideas of her own — ideas he couldn't possibly have considered.

As soon as she drove into Coynesbury she took the turning for the station, parking as close as possible. Her tummy felt as if dozens of butterflies were batting their wings inside it and she walked away from the car then had to turn back and lock it.

Once on the platform, she asked a porter if the train was on time. He told her it was and continued trundling a trolley loaded with postbags. Was he really fifteen? He looked about twelve. She smiled to herself. That air of expectancy heralding the arrival of a long distance train seemed heightened today. Passengers, spotting the engine in the distance, picked up their bags, some moving along the platform. Charlotte suddenly remembered the last time she'd waited for Robert and began walking briskly towards the platform's furthest end.

Slowly the locomotive snaked towards her. Carriages slid past her until the train ground to a halt, leaving her opposite the guard's van. Doors burst open, releasing the usual mix of civilians, servicemen and women on to the platform. Where was the man she'd come to meet? Then she noticed the tall figure standing outside the front carriage of the train. Her heart missed a beat and her legs felt wobbly as she began walking towards him, slowly at first then faster and faster until she was running to Robert, dodging people but earning black looks as others got in her way.

He leaned on his stick, watching her approach, his eyes wary. She knew her first reaction would be important. He looked to be all in one piece but this wasn't the moment for questions.

Her greeting stuck in her throat. All she could do was stop, walk up to him and put her arms around him. As she felt his arms close around her, she rested her head on his shoulder and they stood, holding each other, letting the shouts, banging doors and piercing whistle noise wash over them.

He released her gently, used his stick as support and kissed her lightly on the lips. Still neither said a word.

'Just that one suitcase?' Her voice quavered.

He shot her a resigned smile. 'I'm back in Civvy Street now. Travelling light . . . oh, Charlotte.'

She took both his hands. 'Shall I take you straight home?'

'No,' he said. 'Not ready for that yet. Could we find somewhere to sit? Maybe get a drink? I have a little money.'

Her heart felt as if it would burst. 'I know just the place,' she said.

They sat in the Lyons' Corner House for an hour, eating Madeira cake spread with dark red jam and drinking cups of strong tea. Robert's face contained a touch more colour now. Charlotte, shocked at his gaunt appearance, made no mention of what he'd gone through nor did he seem to want to discuss his experiences.

She brought him up to date, told him her father had taken up the reins again. Eleanor was living back in her flat and the two were contemplating matrimony.

Robert smiled and nodded.

She told him Don was still stationed in India. Robert nodded, his face concerned.

'Pearl volunteered and she's a WAAF

now,' Charlotte said. 'Stationed somewhere in England, doing important things.'

Robert laughed out loud. 'That'll suit her. Did she give Phil his marching orders?'

'Thankfully, yes,' said Charlotte, relieved to see a little of the sparkle back in her fiancé's eyes. 'I'll tell you as much as I know about it but maybe we should go home now. You've had a long day.'

He shrugged. 'I've spent most of it sitting down.' He reached for her hand and held it between his, turning it and looking down at her ring. 'You didn't get much of a bargain,' he said.

'I don't understand.' She wondered how much her heart could endure.

'Charlotte, I'm damaged goods. I've lost the sight in my right eye and I'll probably walk with a limp for the rest of my life. I'm no good for active service. I'm no good to you.'

'Thanks a lot,' she said. 'Are you giving me my marching orders?'

His eyelids fluttered but he kept hold of her hands. 'I'm giving you the chance to walk away, if you wish.'

'Welcome home, Robert,' she said calmly. 'Bear with me, a moment.'

She withdrew her hands from his, rose from the table then dropped to her knees beside him. 'Listen to me, darling,' she said. 'Unless you're suffering from concussion, may I remind you we're still engaged to be married? I haven't stopped wanting to be your wife. Do you still want to marry me?'

For the second time in her life, Charlotte experienced sudden total silence as customers realised a drama was being played out.

'Well, do you?' She still knelt beside her fiancé.

'You know I do.'

'Well, that's all right then.' She scrambled to her feet and looked down at herself. 'Oh, my goodness, Auntie El's going to kill me. I've laddered her best nylon stockings.'

Laughter and clapping greeted the

announcement. A woman blew her nose loudly. To Charlotte's acute embarrassment, an American airman heading for the door dropped a pack of nylon stockings beside her plate. 'Have these on me, Ma'am,' he said. 'Have a nice life, guys.'

On the way home, Charlotte made Robert aware of possibilities for the business, to help cement the family's position.

'We're all one family now, Robert. We look after one another. And that'll apply when Don and Pearl come home.'

He'd been glancing sideways at her. 'You really think we could make a go of it? Make a living for us all?'

'I'm convinced of it. This rotten war won't go on forever. There'll be changes ahead. Dad thinks more and more people will want to buy motorcars. It might take a while but he's keen to expand by running a car dealership. There'll be work for you and Don and for Pearl and me. We need to have faith, Robert.'

'Surely there's not enough space?'

'There is at Fun Land. Your father can hardly wait to tell you all about it.'

For a moment she feared she'd sprung too much on him at once. She slowed down, ready to drive through the open double doors of the Corner Garage.

When she switched off the engine, she took a deep breath and turned to look at him.

His smile told her all she needed to know.

THE END

We do hope that you have enjoyed reading this large print book.

Did you know that all of our titles are available for purchase?

We publish a wide range of high quality large print books including:
Romances, Mysteries, Classics
General Fiction
Non Fiction and Westerns

Special interest titles available in large print are:
The Little Oxford Dictionary
Music Book, Song Book
Hymn Book, Service Book

Also available from us courtesy of Oxford University Press:
Young Readers' Dictionary
(large print edition)
Young Readers' Thesaurus
(large print edition)

For further information or a free brochure, please contact us at:
Ulverscroft Large Print Books Ltd.,
The Green, Bradgate Road, Anstey,
Leicester, LE7 7FU, England.
Tel: (00 44) **0116 236 4325**
Fax: (00 44) **0116 234 0205**

Other titles in the
Linford Romance Library:

YOUR SECRET SMILE

Suzanne Ross Jones

When Sean left town to go travelling, he took a piece of Grace's heart with him. It's taken years for her to get over him and at last she's reached a place where she's happy on her own. Her time is filled with good friends and fulfilling work as a maths teacher. But when Sean reappears as an art teacher at Grace's school, it's obvious he's intent on causing havoc in her well-ordered life.

ACCIDENT PRONE

Anna Ramsay

From hospital ward sister to sanatorium sister at Ditchingham Prep School is a drastic change, but Ruth Silke needs something different. Working with Dr Daniel Gather, the local GP who covers the school, isn't so easy — particularly when he seems all too matter-of-fact about his young son Danny, a boarder at the school. Ruth is convinced that Danny's accidents are a cry for help, but how to persuade Dan? Particularly when their own relationship leaves so much to be desired . . .